"You'd better be careful."

Jake added, "The sun here is fierce and you'll soon fry, with that white skin of yours."

Sass met his eyes in the mirror. "Thanks for the warning, but I've come prepared for things to be pretty hot down here."

He knew she wasn't just talking about the sun.

"Wise," he said. "Foreigners get burned very quickly."

Jake thought he saw her eyebrows arch slightly, a smile of challenge flitting across her face, but it might have only been the effect of sun and shadow from the overhanging trees flashing past.

"Don't you worry about me, Mr. Finlayson. I can take care of myself."

Dear Reader,

This book was conceived in friendship. I grew up in Zimbabwe with my two best friends. We laughed and squabbled and shared all through our childhood and teenage years. Now one lives in Houston, the other in Tulsa and I'm in New Zealand.

I want to write books that link our lives. This story is the first of hopefully many where Americans and Kiwis meet and fall in love—and encounter many obstacles, misunderstandings and adventures along the way.

Having always been a fan of Westerns, visiting Texas was a dream come true, and I was sure I could detect cowboy DNA in those long-legged men and women with their slow, lilting voices. I was especially touched by Texan warmth and generosity. Sass, my heroine, has the same mixture of intelligence, Southern charm and underlying resilience that I encountered there.

Sparks often fly when people from different countries meet. It's not always comfortable, but it is always vivid. I wanted to capture that flare when Sass first confronts Jake, a big wave surfer and typically laconic Kiwi male. Going to another country is also unbalancing and it's good for my headstrong heroine to have her world tilted—especially as she's busy turning Jake's completely upside down.

I had lots of fun writing this U.S./N.Z. book—checking out what makes us different, what makes us the same. I hope you enjoy reading it.

Zana Bell

P.S. I love to hear from readers, so visit me at www.zanabell.com.

P.P.S. And yes, N.Z. truly is fairy-tale beautiful. Even after living here for many years, it still takes my breath away.

Tempting the Negotiator

Zana Bell

TORONTO • NEW YORK • LONDON
AMSTERDAM • PARIS • SYDNEY • HAMBURG
STOCKHOLM • ATHENS • TOKYO • MILAN • MADRID
PRAGUE • WARSAW • BUDAPEST • AUCKLAND

Recycling programs for this product may not exist in your area.

ISBN-13: 978-0-373-78370-0

TEMPTING THE NEGOTIATOR

This edition published by arrangement with Harlequin Books S.A.

For questions and comments about the quality of this book please contact us at Customer_eCare@Harlequin.ca.

www.eHarlequin.com

Printed in U.S.A.

ABOUT THE AUTHOR

Zana Bell was born and raised in Zimbabwe, which she left in her early twenties in search of adventure. Her travels ended abruptly a few years later when she came to New Zealand, fell in love with a Kiwi and stayed. The daughter of British parents and the mother of Kiwi children, she delights in the misunderstandings, laughter and insights that occur when nationalities and cultures mix. She lives with a mountain at her back and a harbor before her, a constant source of joy.

To Geoff, Zoe, Tayga and Whanau

With thanks to the Whangarei branches of the New Zealand Ornithological Society and Department of Conservation for giving me their time and support regarding the fairy tern.

CHAPTER ONE

TRYING TO IGNORE the high thrum of the airplane engine, Sass leaned back against her seat and shut her eyes. She'd forced her shoulders into a semblance of relaxation but her hands remained clenched in her lap. Only another ten minutes.

"Feeling sick?"

Sass opened her eyes and looked into the sympathetic face of the woman across the tiny aisle. She tried to smile.

"I don't like flying too much."

Sass Walker was a terra firma kinda gal. She liked to feel the earth beneath her feet, preferably with a comforting layer of asphalt. She also liked maps and lists. Fine print was her forte, which made her great at her job. She liked order and control. Especially control. And right now this tin can of an airplane didn't feel at all controlled. Neither did her life.

The woman smiled. "Don't worry. It's really very safe."

The six-seater sure didn't feel it. Sass bet that if she punched the side, her fist would go right through.

"Besides, we're nearly there," the woman continued. "See, there's the harbor coming into view right now."

Every one of the six passengers had a window seat, and Sass forced herself to look out. Most people, she knew, would have been spellbound by the generous antipodean harbor surrounded by shaggy green mountains, but she was horribly jet-lagged and still smarting from life's unfairness.

"American?"

Sass nodded. She saw the woman's gaze travel down her caramel Prada suit to her black Christian Louboutin pumps with their trademark red soles.

"I know who you are! You're the lawyer come to set up the tourist resort in Aroha Bay."

The heavy-jowled man diagonally in front of Sass spun around. "Come to destroy the bay, more like!"

"Oh, come off it, Reg, the town could do with a boost to its economy and you know it."

Inwardly Sass groaned. It was starting already, the dissidence she was here to calm. Kurt the Incompetent had ballsed up big-time, rushing in with multimillion-dollar schemes without consultation, without checking the facts, and now she'd been sent in to clean up the mess. And while she was exiled here at the Back-of-Beyond at the bottom of the world, Kurt would be smarming his way into the promotion she'd been killing herself with eighty-hour weeks, years on end, to win. All her frustration, her fury, now turned on New Zealand, though Sass was careful to smile.

"I'm just here to listen to what all you folks have to say. My company is concerned to discover there's local opposition to what they thought would be a wonderful business opportunity for Whangarimu."

"And it is!" the woman agreed.

The man scowled. "We don't need Americans coming in and taking over. It's a bloody disgrace. Did you see the plans? Amazon ruins in the middle of New Zealand forests? What did he call it—Jungle Paradise? Utter tosh."

The man had a point. Sass herself had been speechless when Kurt had unveiled his brainchild back in New York. Paradise Resorts prided itself on its theme-based holiday locations, and Kurt had seen the New Zealand forest as the perfect setting for a Mayan complex topped by a large "temple" casino.

The plane's shrill engine changed tone as it began its descent. Sass was deeply relieved to see the airport below; grateful not to have to continue the discussion any longer, grateful that this interminable trip of nearly thirty hours was over. She craved the silence of a hotel room, a hot shower and a glass of chilled white wine. Most of all she craved a cigarette.

Touchdown was soft, and within seconds the pilot had flung open the door of the plane and lowered the stairs.

"Welcome to Whangarimu!"

Knees wobbly, she stepped out of the plane. The brilliant late afternoon sunlight was like a slap in the face. She walked across the small runway toward a one-level building she assumed was the airport. Several people were gathered, waiting to greet the arrivals, and she searched for someone holding up a card with her name on it, Kurt having assured her she'd be met. Nada. Great, just great. She began to make her way to the counter when a hand on her arm waylaid her.

"Sass Walker?"

She didn't know who she'd been expecting, but certainly hadn't pictured a man who could tower over her, even when she was wearing her highest heels. She also hadn't expected such breadth of shoulders under his faded T-shirt or the green eyes, so startling against the tanned face.

"Yes?"

"I'm Jake Finlayson."

Surprised and very wary, she asked, "As in

one of the Finlayson brothers spearheading the protests?"

"That's right."

She took in his battered surf shorts, his tawny, salt-encrusted curls. His long legs. He must be the one who'd upended the scale model Kurt had presented at a town meeting three weeks earlier. The one who'd thrown Kurt out of the hall. The reason she'd been sent in Kurt's place.

"An act of lunacy," Kurt had explained to The Boys. "This Finlayson is a deadbeat surfer who rents a house on Aroha Beach. Nothing to worry about, he's a nobody."

Though it was amazing how quickly this nobody and his lawyer brother had whipped together enough ecological concerns to keep Paradise Resorts tied up in legal battles for months if not years. Was this guy here to bundle her back onto the airplane?

"I'm here to take you to your accommodation."

His voice betrayed no emotion, but he radiated hostility, and Sass was damned if she was going anywhere with a man who'd threatened to emasculate her colleague—however much he deserved it.

"That's very kind of you, Mr. Finlayson," she said brightly, "but don't you worry, I can manage by myself. If you tell me the name of my hotel, I'll take a cab."

The Kiwi raised one eyebrow. "Hotel? We were informed that you were insistent on staying out at Aroha Bay, despite the lack of facilities. Of course, seeing as your company owns the land now, you are entitled to be there."

Kurt! He was really out to get her on this trip. Already he'd failed to give her the files, with apologies for a crashed computer. He'd briefed her quickly, of course, but she knew he'd been holding out on her. He wasn't about to let her succeed where he'd failed.

Sass smiled tautly. "Seems like wires got crossed somewhere over the Pacific, Mr. Finlayson, but hey, no problem. I'll book into whichever hotel has a vacancy."

"Call me Jake. We don't stand on ceremony in New Zealand. I don't see what the problem is. Branston," he said, making the name sound like a swearword, "was explicit that you would be staying in the sleep-out at my house. It's right on the beach where you want to build your resort. He said you were very keen on getting the full ambience of the place."

Sarcasm and accusation were equally balanced. For a second Sass could only stare as the full extent of Kurt's perfidy dawned on her. He was sending her straight into the lion's den. Looking up at the implacable face in front of her, Sass saw that Kurt had, at the same time, revenged himself on his enemy, too. As low-down, dirty tricks went, it was pretty inspired.

Jake frowned. "Look, if you've changed your mind—"

"No, not at all."

She couldn't afford to seem indecisive, would have to bluff through for the moment, the best she could. Just wait till she got her hands on that conniving son of a bitch, though.

"That's fine," she added. "Of course it is. Great. Now, where's the baggage claim?"

"It's in the shed out back. I'll take you."

He led her around the tiny airport building to a shed where, in the gloom, she saw the other passengers sorting through the pile of luggage on a trolley.

"Which one's yours?" he asked. She pointed and he swung the large suitcase off easily. "Good, follow me."

"Wait. There's also that one, and that bag, too."

He didn't need to say anything; his expression said it all as he scooped up her other luggage. Well, she thought defensively, who knew how long she was going to be here? Also, not knowing what setup she was coming to, she'd packed outfits to suit every occasion. He didn't need to look like that!

Her current outfit, however, didn't fit this occasion. Jake led her to an open-topped Jeep where a large dog of indeterminate lineage presided in the front seat, tongue hanging out with the heat. Jake walked to the back of the vehicle, shifted a surfboard to one side and began throwing her suitcases in. Exhausted and bad-tempered as she was, Sass couldn't help noticing his easy athleticism. In another situation she might have found him attractive, sexy even, in a rumpled, outdoor man kinda way. But Sass never mixed business and pleasure. Besides, this guy was dangerous.

"I can move Gerty to the backseat if you like, but she leaves a shocking mess of hairs behind her. You might not want to get them on your clothes. It's your call."

Again, there was nothing overtly hostile in his manner, but Sass knew he resented her almost as much as she resented this whole damned country.

"No problem, I'll take the backseat."

It was a challenge. Sass pulled her tight skirt halfway up her thighs to scramble in. She wished she hadn't changed in Auckland, but it was her creed never to be seen tousled or crumpled. Her immaculate appearance was one of her strongest weapons—and defenses.

Jake swung himself into the front seat and

adjusted the rearview mirror slightly. He surveyed her, his eyes cool, green and unwavering, like a knight staring through the visor of his helmet. Yet there were laughter lines, too. As she wriggled, trying to pull her skirt down to her knees, Sass wondered what he looked like when he smiled. The backseat was scorching and the seat belt metal burned as she buckled herself in. Her eyes were scratchy from the long flight and she narrowed them against the glare. Damned sunglasses were in her other bag.

In silence, they drove out of the airport and came almost immediately to a T-junction where the left-hand sign read, Whangarimu City Centre and the right-hand sign read, Whangarimu Heads. They turned right.

JAKE WATCHED HER PROFILE as she took in the scenery, and wondered how it would strike a stranger. The road hugged the contours of the harbor, threading through the myriad bays, each rimmed by a horseshoe of modest homes and with a cluster of small yachts bobbing on the late-afternoon tide. A seagull wheeled above with its hoarse, stuttering cry, and Jake's stomach churned at the thought of developers coming in to ruin it all. He blamed the *Lord of the Rings* movies for alerting developers from all over the world to the beauty of New Zealand. Locals didn't stand a chance against foreign currency, and coastal properties advertised on the Internet were now being snapped up at insane prices. That American braggart had bought Aroha Bay for a few million dollars in one brief visit. Money no object. People, place, nature of no concern. Well, Jake had got rid of him but it seemed the Americans were using a different sort of attack now. Easier on the eye, but this lady gave nothing away.

"Those are nice," Sass said, nodding at the huge, ancient trees that reached sprawling, gnarled branches out over the water's edge. Her accent was warm and made him think absurdly of honeysuckle and soft summer nights.

"They're pohutukawa. We call them our Christmas tree because they have red flowers in December."

"They're really something." Her hand was halfway to her handbag. "Mind if I smoke?"

"I do, actually. I hate the smell of smoke in the car."

Their eyes locked. The wind was whipping her long hair about her head, and the smell of dog punctuated the air. He knew she knew he was just being contrary.

"No problem," she said, and sat back, breaking eye contact and looking out over the water as though she didn't give a damn. It gave him a chance to examine her. Nobody should look that good after a thirty-hour flight. Her eyes were so blue, he wondered if she wore colored contact lenses. She had delicate bones, white-blond hair and a fair complexion.

"You'd better be careful," he said. "The sun here is fierce and you'll soon fry with that white skin of yours."

Her eyes met his. "Thanks for the warning, but I've come prepared for things to be pretty hot down here."

He knew she wasn't talking about the sun.

"Wise," he said. "Foreigners get burned very quickly."

Jake thought he saw her eyebrows arch slightly, a smile of challenge flitting across her face, but it might only have been the effect of sun and shadow from the overhanging trees flashing past.

"Don't you worry about me, Mr. Finlayson. I can take care of myself."

With that, she captured her flying hair and somehow twisted it into a knot, untidy but tamed.

"Jake," he corrected. "Where's your name come from? I've never met a Sass before."

"It's a nickname from Sasha."

"As in sassy?" he hazarded.

She laughed. "No, as in pain in the proverbial.

I had two younger brothers who resented their bossy older sister. Our mom didn't allow cussing."

Their gazes met again. For a second he saw humor glimmer in her eyes, then Jake looked back at the road. He wasn't about to start liking her—Miss Pain-in-the.

They fell silent, and instead of trying for more lame conversation, he switched on the stereo, letting the Chili Peppers take them down the length of the harbor. Just as they were about to swing onto the dirt road leading to Aroha Bay, she called out, "Stop."

It sounded like *"Staap."* Jake pulled over and waited as the lawyer took stock. It was, he resentfully acknowledged, an idyllic location for a resort. The Jeep sat on the top of a long, narrow ridge that flattened and rounded into a small peninsula, ending in a long sand spit. The view was almost three-sixty, looking down the harbor on the right-hand side and over the open ocean on the left. It would suit all types of holiday-makers. Aroha Bay below them was flat and tranquil, offering safe swimming all year round. On the seaward side, waves unfurled with lazy uniformity right along the coast. On both sides pohutukawa clung to the cliff faces while flax bushes fanned the sands. The only sign of habitation was his dilapidated house near the beach. Jake wondered what Sass saw—the bay as it was now or some future travesty of it in her head.

"Aroha Bay is a pretty name. What does it mean?"

"*Aroha* is the Māori word for love." He sounded curt, but couldn't help it.

She just nodded and asked, "What's that?" pointing to where the ridge ended in a hill with grassy terraces.

"The pā—an old Māori fortification. Māori used to have pā up and down the coast, but this one is particularly significant."

"Oh?" It was hard to read her expression. "Kurt never mentioned it."

"He was too busy finding out where the nearest nightclub is."

Jake saw Sass give a faint, disparaging smile—no love lost between those two, then—and wondered why the pā site had caught her attention. Most visitors barely noticed it.

"Shall we go?" he asked at length.

She drew her eyes away, clearly pulling her thoughts back to the present. "Sure."

Jake spun the wheels a little as he took off, and ground the gears as they drove the last kilometer down the steep, rutted track to the bay. Bringing the enemy right into the heart of paradise.

CHAPTER TWO

SASS'S HEART SANK as they drew up in a whirl of dust between a run-down old house and what appeared to be a shed. It was nothing like the hotel room she'd been hoping for.

"This is the sleep-out," said Jake, leaping from the Jeep and waving at the shed. "You'll be comfortable here, I hope."

There was not an ounce of sincerity in what he said. Wordlessly, Sass wriggled out of the backseat and dropped onto her heels, which immediately embedded themselves in the dusty driveway. Jake hauled out her bags and led her up the steps onto the deck of the "sleep-out" and into the room.

It might have been a shed once, but now its walls were painted a pale yellow that echoed the late-afternoon sun. The front wall had been replaced with glass doors that overlooked the grassy reaches of the garden to the sun-spangled bay beyond. The view was a million bucks, but the furniture had a knock-kneed look. There were no drapes at the windows. The place was big but smelled musty.

"Here's the bathroom," he said, opening a door to the side. "You can use the house's kitchen. I was going to move some of the boys out here but thought you'd prefer to have some privacy with five blokes around."

"Five!"

He smiled at her shock. "It's a bit of a bad boys' home—not that the kids are bad as such, just a little wild. They're with me for six months as an experiment in early intervention."

His tone implied that a lawyer might not understand the concept, but she glanced at him in surprise. Jake didn't look like a social worker. In fact, he seemed a little wild himself with his tangle of tawny curls. There was an exotic slant to his high cheekbones and a honey tone to his deep tan. His legs were long and muscular—*not an office worker,* she decided. The battered shorts were, of course, another clue.

She looked around. "Can I get on the Internet here?"

Jake shook his head. "Sorry, I've never bothered getting it. Cell phones are pretty useless, too, most of the time. Reception is patchy. You can get all that in Whangarimu, though. Come on, I'll show you the house. Like a cup of tea?"

"I'd love a coffee if that's okay."

"American. Of course."

Sass was impressed. There was nothing in his tone, but she'd just been insulted. Silently, she followed him to the house, her heels sinking into the shaggy lawn.

The building had excellent bones, with a wood exterior and deep veranda. Going inside, however, was like walking into Man Zone. The lounge was beautiful, with French doors and a generous windowseat in the eastern wall, but it was cluttered with sagging furniture and DVDs and PlayStation games. A large television and Xbox dominated one corner. The dining room had a huge table sadly in need of a polish and buried in books and papers.

In the kitchen, cupboards hung open, dishes were piled in the sink. The breakfast things were on the table. For a brief, horrible moment Sass flashed back to the chaos of the trailer home she'd grown up in, a far cry from the immaculate order she surrounded herself with these days.

"Place is a bit of a tip, I'm afraid," Jake said, not sounding the least apologetic. "Now, coffee, did you say?"

She looked around for his coffee machine as he

put the kettle on. Then she watched as he opened a tin of instant, chipped at it for a second—God, how old was it?—then heaped a teaspoon of lumps into what she was relieved to see appeared to be a clean mug.

"Where are the kids now?"

"Should be back from school any minute, but they won't stop to talk—the waves are too good. They're all mad keen surfers. That's why they're with me. They're preparing for the nationals and this location is unbeatable. Milk? No—just black? There you are, pull up a chair if you like."

"No thanks, I'll take the coffee over to the sh—sleep-out?—and start settling in if you don't mind."

"Suit yourself. Dinner around eight okay for you?"

She shook her head and put on a smile. "That's kind, but no thanks. I'm beat. I'd like to have an early night."

It was true she felt light-headed with exhaustion, but there was also no way she was going to eat anything out of that kitchen till she'd had time to fumigate the house. Coffee mug in hand, she began heading out, her system singing in anticipation of a cigarette.

"One more thing. This is a smoke-free zone. Several of the boys have quit. I'm sure you understand."

She turned to look at him. He looked back.

"Sure," she said slowly, her fingers tightening on the mug. "I understand."

Back in her quarters she kicked off her heels with vehemence, opened her bag and for a second gazed longingly at her cigarettes. Later, when they were all eating dinner, she would sneak one behind the sleep-out. From under her cigarettes she pulled out her BlackBerry. Sure enough, no reception. *Great.* The toughest challenge of her career and here she was, stuck in the remotest corner of the bottom of the world with no line out.

Sass was good at her job, damned good. Some called her The Great Persuader, others The Great Manipulator. Whichever, she was the original fix-it gal. But she'd had to work twice as hard and be three times better than any male colleague just to be noticed. For seven years, Sass had given her life to her job, her sole goal being to one day make senior partner, aka join The Boys who ran Paradise Resorts. Her break had finally come last week when she'd been summonsed to Mr. Brixby's office.

For the first time since she'd started at the company, he'd led her to the sofas in the corner instead of consulting over his desk. They'd sat and he'd looked her right in the eye.

"Sass, we are sending you to New Zealand. I'll be honest with you. Profits are down and the company desperately needs the injection from a new resort. Something fresh. I know," he said, raising his hand as Sass went to speak, "Branston's idea is fanciful. But we need something that will make people sit up, take note. We need a new direction and we're all counting on you to make it work. Will you do this for us, Sass?"

And Sass, contrary to her usual thoroughness in checking out details beforehand, had looked back into those shrewd eyes and said, "Why of course, Mr. Brixby."

He'd even patted her hand. "I knew we could rely on you. Your level thinking and charm might make all the difference."

He didn't say outright that this might secure her place with The Boys in the vacancy McKenna's retirement had left, but the way he'd said it… Her heart had leaped and his words had continued to warm and sustain her right up until she'd seen Kurt's smirk. Then she'd realized he believed she stood no chance at all, and that she'd take the rap for his enormous blunders. Worse, while she was trapped in this black hole, he'd be right there, ingratiating himself with The Boys.

Unable to stand being inside, she wandered out, down the steps of the deck toward the beach.

Walking barefoot on grass brought back memories of racing late to school, playing catch…and it felt strangely good. She drifted to the ragged edge of the lawn and down the bank onto the sand. That felt good, too. She wrapped her fingers around her mug of coffee, took a sip, then grimaced. That was another thing she needed. Already she was making a shopping list in her mind.

The water was wonderful and she stood ankle-deep, feeling her frustrations ebb into the sea. The sun was gentler now, sinking low in the sky, and she raised her face to it. She hadn't just stood, enjoying the feeling of sun and water, for who knew how long. She breathed in deeply, eyes closed, the salty tang carrying the whisper of romance and exotica.

Her eyes snapped open. She was most certainly not here on holiday, and she pulled her thoughts back to the ridge behind her, with its pa. Was that why Kurt had been so happy to off-load this deal onto her? What a mess. She'd have to watch her step closely if she was going to succeed.

Her host's casual appearance didn't deceive her. She'd seen the stubborn lines around his mouth, had noted the pugilistic set of his jaw. In the past Jake would have been in the front line of battle; with his height and reckless determination he would have led the men behind him and intimidated those he faced. Well, she wasn't about to be intimidated. All the same, she needed to tread very carefully. If he caught one whiff of what she knew, then the deal—and her whole future—would be toast!

CHAPTER THREE

"LAST MAN HOME MAKES breakfast," yelled Brad as he leaped down the hill from the ridge. The rest of the boys broke into a run, chasing him with whoops and threats, their surfboards bouncing and swinging as they raced.

Jake let them go, glad to have this moment to himself. Dawn had broken while they were out on the water, turning the waves pink and yellow, and now he breathed in, enjoying the soft salt tang. The sky was translucent blue and the harbor stretched out in tranquil high tide. It was unthinkable that this early morning peace and beauty, unchanged for a thousand years, should now be threatened.

The boys, still whooping, had disappeared around the corner of the house when, inexplicably, their cries died midyell. Curious, Jake loped down the steep driveway, and as he rounded the house, saw what had silenced them. Sass, in a black swimsuit, had emerged from the sea and was making her way slowly up the beach toward them. Brad whistled under his breath; Paul gulped. The twins blushed red and exchanged abashed, sideways grins. Jake couldn't blame them. Though her swimsuit was modestly cut, it molded to her. Clearly, they grew them tall and lithe in Texas, with long legs that could— Jake swiftly blocked the highly inappropriate thoughts that crowded into his mind. An understandable reaction, he told himself. The natural response of a year's self-enforced celibacy.

She smiled, but Jake was surprised to see her pause as though unsure, shy even, as she eyed the lineup of young males.

"Hey, you must be the gang Jake spoke of."

"Yeah," said Jake, collecting himself. "The lanky one is Paul, the twins Mike and Mark—don't worry if you can't tell them apart, no one can—and Brad's the one with his tongue hanging out."

Brad threw him a look as he shifted his board to his other arm and held out a hand. "Pleased to meet you." His formal manner, however, was undermined by the thoughts so clearly written all over his adolescent face.

Sass moved forward and Paul swallowed again as she shook Brad's hand. "I'm Sass. Pleased to meet y'all."

Then she turned to shake the other boys' hands, spellbinding each in turn with her smile, which, Jake had to grudgingly admit, was friendly and in no way playing up the obvious effect she was having on them all.

"Nice swim?" he asked.

"Yes, the water was lovely. I woke early—jet lag I guess—and it looked so inviting I couldn't resist. How was the surf?" Her Southern voice floated lazy and warm, complementing the early morning air.

"It was awesome! Do you surf?" Brad asked.

She shook her head. "I almost never went to the sea when I was a child, and I live in New York now. Closest I've ever got has been watching *First Break.*"

"We can teach you, can't we, Jake?"

But Sass just smiled. "I don't think so, thanks. I'm a flat water gal. But I'd sure like to see you in action sometime."

"We need some action now. Showers and breakfast pronto." Jake sounded more abrupt than he'd intended, but seeing her bewitch his boys, he felt absurdly betrayed. Only last night they'd all been so indignant at the mere thought of a New York lawyer. "We're going into town soon and if you aren't ready by the time we leave, you'll have to stay home, clean the house and miss out on the paintball."

The threat worked. In seconds the boys said hasty farewells, dropped their boards and disappeared into the house, forming a bottleneck at the door as they fought to be first to the shower. Jake shook his head, but Sass laughed. "They remind me of my brothers."

He had forgotten she'd mentioned having brothers. He'd imagined she must have sprung fully grown from some Mattel factory, a perfect Barbie. "I hope they weren't like that disreputable horde."

Sass's face was unreadable—no wonder she was a hotshot lawyer. "Mmm," was all she said before asking, "Am I going to meet your brother today?"

"Yeah, if you don't mind working on a Saturday."

"On the contrary, I'm really looking forward to it."

Jake just bet she was—looking forward to racing things through, just like that Branston bastard had.

"Fine, I'll drive you in. What time suits you?"

"The earlier, the better. We've a lot to get through."

Jake had never known anyone could sound so brisk and businesslike in clinging Lycra. He saw the fine hairs on her arms rise in the early morning breeze.

"You'd better hop into a shower yourself. The

sleep-out has its own tank, so you'll have plenty of hot water. How about we meet in an hour—does that give you enough time?"

"More than enough, thank you." Her voice was still polite, but had cooled a few degrees with the boys' departure.

"Help yourself to breakfast, as well," he added.

"Thanks, but I usually skip it. I'll see you in an hour."

SASS CHOSE HER OUTFIT with care. No heels, she realized now. No suits. Well, that eliminated half her luggage. No one had warned her of just how informal these Kiwis were, and she certainly didn't want to put their backs up. At the same time she wanted to make sure they knew she wasn't a pushover, either. In the end she opted for black trousers and a soft white shirt she'd hung up the night before, along with several other options. It was still a little crumpled, but she had absolutely no intention of letting Jake see her iron.

Makeup and hair also required thought. She kept the former to a minimum, just enough to enhance her eyes and lose that soft, girlie look she despised. She glossed her lips with a subtle no-nonsense red, then tied her hair back into a French roll. Finally, she selected a pair of black pumps with unmistakable Italian chic that only had a slight heel.

It wasn't easy to see the overall effect in the small mirror tacked to the wall, but having twisted this way and that, Sass decided it was probably good enough. Drawing in a deep breath, she ran her hands down her sides. This was it.

The first meeting was crucial. As with runners before a race, so much of the final outcome lay in the first confrontation. Her whole future hinged on this. Blow this one and she blew her shot at the top.

The unwelcome image of Kurt's smug smile flashed through her brain, and her fingers curled into a fist. No way! How smart could these guys be, anyway?

But even as she braced herself with this tough talk, she was bothered by the image of Jake as she'd seen him half an hour earlier—with the water beading on his tanned biceps and pecs, his curls flattened from his swim but already beginning to spring up again as though refusing to be tamed. His long legs and the glimpse of flat abs, mostly hidden by the board, had done something to her stomach. She was in no mood to wonder exactly what.

Standing there, wearing only surf shorts, he'd still looked to be one of the most dangerous men she'd ever seen, despite the unexpected charm of his smile. Not that he smiled much. Well, not at her, at any rate. *Good.* She didn't want to be friends, either. She wanted to allay fears, clinch the deal and get the hell out of here.

"Go get them, girl!" she told herself, although she'd never really been the cheerleader sort. Picking up her briefcase as though it were a shield, she stepped out into the sun.

THIS TIME THEY TRAVELED in a beat-up old van, with the boys sprawled in the backseats. Sass had to smile. The twins shared an iPod, with an earpiece each, while Brad was immersed in playing games on his cell phone. Paul sat right at the back, staring out the window, lost in his own world.

Sass turned to look at the stern profile beside her. "I hope your brother doesn't mind meeting on a Saturday," Sass said to break the awkward silence.

"Not at all. No doubt you'll have been filled in on the major objections to the resort, but Rob thought it might be helpful to have a chat before the town meeting on Tuesday night."

They wanted to check her out. "Sure, it's an excellent idea. I'm keen to meet him, too. He's a lawyer, right? Does he work for a big firm?"

Jake shook his head. The sun was streaming in his side of the car, backlighting his curls. His elbow rested on the open window and the hairs on his arm glinted gold. His eyes were very slightly narrowed, but Sass wasn't sure if that was because of the sun. Her own sunglasses were opaque and she took advantage of this to check him out. He must have dressed up for the occasion, she concluded. The shorts had been replaced by battered jeans that sat snugly on his hips. A crumpled, short-sleeved green shirt was loosely tucked in—a concession to formality, maybe.

"Rob's gone independent," he said.

It figured. Sass guessed that independence would be pretty important to both Finlayson brothers.

"Brave," she said. "Gets rid of office politics, but probably produces other challenges."

Did the laughter lines around his eyes crinkle or was that still just the sun? "Yeah, dirty nappies for a start. Rob works from home so he and Moana can share child care."

Her heart rose. A part-time lawyer sounded ideal. How hard could this be? Then she looked at Jake's long jawline and uncompromising chin, and felt her heart flutter back down again. Still, she kept her tone light and easy.

"Really? It must get tricky balancing everything. Is she a lawyer, too?"

Jake shook his head again. To give the guy some credit, he seemed oblivious to how good his curls looked tossed about in the sun. If it'd been Kurt, she'd have known he was doing it for effect.

"She's a psychologist and uses the same office for consultations. It's amazing how they manage, but it seems to work."

Jake and Sass fell into silence again and he flicked on the radio. A Haydn violin concerto filled the car, surprising her and drawing protests from the boys. Jake ignored them, and the muttering soon died away.

The music was turned up loud, hiding the rumbling of her stomach. She was jet-lagged and hungry, but still determined not to avail herself of Jake's hospitality. Thank goodness she'd sneaked a cigarette before her swim.

WHANGARIMU PROVED TO BE an attractive town set at the top of the harbor, where it narrowed into a marina. Restaurants and gift shops lined the water's edge and palm trees made it feel tropical. The center was compact, clustered with small shops that reminded Sass of towns back home before huge shopping malls had taken over. But she also saw that some frontages were nailed up and that there were a number of people just sitting around the marina, looking at the boats. She'd seen that slumped-shouldered lethargy before, in trailer parks, and wondered what the unemployment numbers were.

"Right, hop out," Jake ordered the kids as they

pulled up at a red light. "We'll be a few hours max. I'll text you when we're ready to pick you up. Don't keep me waiting."

The boys scrambled out with hurried goodbyes, and Sass was sorry to see them go. They hadn't eased the conversation, but their mere presence had helped her relax. Without them, the silence in the van seemed to swell.

Fortunately, it was only a few minutes later that the van drew up in front of a cottage painted a jaunty yellow with blue trim. The garden was a tumble of flowers and the overall effect was charming, except Sass wasn't prepared to concede anything at this stage.

"We're here," Jake announced unnecessarily.

He ushered her through the front door and into a tiny office immediately off the hall. A man rose to greet them.

"It's great to meet you," he said, and actually seemed to mean it. "I'm Rob Finlayson."

Rob was also tall, with straight hair and a kinder expression than his brother. He met her eyes and smiled warmly, but she still knew she was being appraised. His handshake was firm and Sass realized that he, like his brother, was not to be underestimated. Instinctively, she liked him.

Unfortunately. She didn't want to like anyone. This resolve was further tested when Moana came in with a wide smile of welcome. Her skin was cinnamon-brown, her hair black and luxuriant, reaching right down her back. Māori, Sass guessed, having done her homework about New Zealand and its indigenous people. Beautiful and exotic, Moana looked as if she'd stepped out of some Hawaiian musical.

"Hi, welcome to New Zealand. Can I get you some coffee? I've also baked some muffins."

The aroma of freshly ground beans had struck Sass the minute she'd walked through the door. "Black coffee and a muffin would be wonderful, thank you."

Not risking the indignity of a growling stomach was even better.

"Two minutes," Moana promised as she slipped away.

Sass avoided Jake's eyes as she took the chair he proffered, and said, "Shall we get straight to business?"

As she set her briefcase on her knee and clicked open the locks she saw the guys exchange glances. Mistake! She'd forgotten time might not mean money here. You might have to put your watch forward seventeen hours upon reaching New Zealand, but it seemed you also had to dial back some years.

"Of course," said Rob. "Would you like to put

your briefcase here?" He pushed papers aside to make space for her.

"Thanks." She drew her chair to the desk, then wished she hadn't. It brought her closer to the brothers, and their combined height and, well, maleness made her uncomfortable. She glanced up in relief when Moana returned with a steaming mug and a plate with the muffin.

"Now, I don't want you ganging up on our visitor. Jake, you come with me. I've a new painting that needs hanging and Rob has been less than no help these past two days."

"I've always said you chose the wrong brother," Jake pointed out. "Rob's the lazy one." Suddenly Sass saw a completely different man—one relaxed with laid-back good humor, and a wicked glint of mischief in his eye.

"She chose the best-looking one," his brother retorted. "Besides, I did try to hang the damned thing but gave up after she changed her mind half a dozen times." He ducked as his wife took a swipe at his head.

"Excuses, excuses, ay." Moana exchanged a woman-to-woman look with Sass. "That's all men really excel in."

Sass couldn't help smiling back, but felt off balance. This wasn't like the business meetings she was used to.

"Right," she said, trying to take control once more by lifting a sheaf of papers from the briefcase and passing them to Rob. "I've some data here that might interest you."

"Good luck," said Jake, though it wasn't clear who he was speaking to. She could almost feel his body heat as he passed behind her chair and disappeared out of the room after Moana. Sass was glad to see his back. With him gone, she'd be able to concentrate.

Rob bent over the projected incomes Paradise resorts expected from their Aroha enterprise, a report that Kurt had prepared.

"You'll see it will bring considerable amounts of money into your community," she pointed out.

He shook his head. "These numbers seem pitched a bit high to me. Not that I'm fully conversant with the resort business, of course."

Sass had also thought they were optimistic, but The Boys had okayed them.

"We have every faith that your beautiful country will attract huge numbers of visitors, given the right advertising. Your weak dollar will also make it affordable for families on modest incomes."

"We try to keep a handle on tourist numbers here in New Zealand. Don't want to spoil our clean green image with hordes tramping over the countryside."

He smiled and she smiled back. The first clash of swords.

"Speaking of which," he continued, "we haven't received full information about the massive infrastructures of roads, water, sewerage, etc., you'll need to install for a resort this size."

"That's all in the pipeline," she said confidently, crossing her fingers. Kurt had been maddeningly vague. "I'll get them to you soon."

"Our biggest concern, however, is the fairy tern."

"The bird. Yeah, right. I understand there are only seven birds nesting on the spit."

"Seven is a considerable number when the bird is listed as severely endangered." Rob's voice had acquired an edge.

"Please believe me my company has no desire whatsoever to hasten this bird's demise." Sass was at her most sincere. "We've looked into options to save it and already have several we'd like to put to you."

"We need Jake for that. He's the expert on the fairy tern. He's writing a book about them."

"Really?" It was hard to think of Action Man reading a book, let alone writing one. She really didn't like the way the guy kept knocking her off-kilter. "Well, as he's not here, let's get back to the resort development." She handed Rob another piece of paper. "You will see here we'll be generating a lot of jobs for the community."

And so the meeting continued for another twenty minutes, with Sass and Rob circling each other as only civilized people locked in legal combat can. By the end, each had developed a healthy respect for the other, but Rob surprised her when he pushed all the papers aside and leaned forward, hands clasped and looked into her eyes. "Sass, would you do one thing for us?"

"I'll try," she said, instantly wary.

"You say you've come to listen, not to steamroll over us. That's a relief and we'd appreciate it if you'd take time to become acquainted with the community and Aroha Bay. Will you do that? We have so much riding on it all."

Me, too, buddy, she thought. *Me, too.*

Her professional smile remained bright. "Sure, I'll be happy to. In fact, I was going to ask, do you have any books about the area? I'd be interested to learn more about the layout of the land and even some of its history. It all helps to get a better picture."

Rob beamed, clearly delighted by her interest. "Yeah, I've got a couple of excellent ones that I'd be delighted to lend you, as a matter of fact."

"Great. I also want to meet with the—" Sass broke off as she flipped through some papers "—the Aroha Bay Organization for Resort Development, the ABORD Committee. I believe they are all for the resort."

Rob grimaced.

"Yeah, well, I'm here to listen to all sides," she continued, "before I make my recommendations. My report to the company will of course be confidential, because in the end the final decision rests with them. Whatever conclusions I come to, they'll be made with due consideration and in everyone's best interests."

As those words slipped out, she experienced a small twinge of conscience. The bottom line was she'd been sent to get these guys to not only accept the resort, but in the end to be glad about it, thus saving her company time and money in court.

"Fair enough." Rob's smile had all the sincerity hers lacked. "Jake will show you around, then."

Her smile froze. "No need. I'll be fine on my own."

"We wouldn't hear of it! New Zealand is not easy to get around in without a car, and there's no better guide than Jake. He knows the land like the back of his hand, plus he can tell you about the birds. He's nuts about them. You guys'll get along well, I know you will."

She smiled again, but inwardly she cursed.

"We can begin at once," Rob continued. "We're

taking Jake's boys to play paintball this afternoon. It'll be the perfect opportunity for you to get to know us in relaxed circumstances."

"Great," she said. "That'll be just great."

IN THE BEDROOM UPSTAIRS, Jake was about to hammer the nail into the wall when Moana said, "Rob told me you have to take this lawyer under your wing."

Jake missed the nail and hit his thumb. He cursed and flicked his hand furiously. "He wants me to *what?*"

Moana picked up the nail and handed it to Jake, who glowered, but turned back to the job. "C'mon Jake, we've got to win her over. If it comes to a head-on confrontation, we'll lose. They have far more money than we'll ever have and will bankrupt us by playing it out over months, even years. We've got to be sneaky. Woo her."

Jake snorted. "That's highly unlikely. I've never encountered such a cold customer in my life."

Three brisk raps and the nail was half driven into the wall. He really wanted to bang it all the way in.

Moana nudged him to one side, hung the picture, then stepped back to admire it, head cocked. "What's the big deal? She seems fine to me. All you have to do is be nice. Show her the birds. They're so cute she'll love them. Take her swimming and surfing. If she falls in love with Aroha Bay then she's bound to come on our side."

Jake ran his fingers through his hair. "It's not that simple. We've already got off on the wrong foot."

"How?" Moana looked at him in surprise.

He shrugged. "It was hate at first sight. There's no chemistry between us. Besides, I'm way too busy with the book and everything right at this moment. Get someone else to show her around."

"Who? Rob and I are tied up with the baby. Sass is so gorgeous that Pete'll try to flirt, while Alison'll murder her if we leave them alone two minutes."

"Yeah, Allie's really committed to the terns."

"Especially since you came on the scene..." Moana smiled as she saw his expression. "Okay, don't believe me! Getting back to this lawyer, it'll only be for a week. You may even grow to like each other."

"What? Me and Miss Pain-in-the?" He laughed. "That's never going to happen."

CHAPTER FOUR

"OKAY, WE NEED TEAMS. Rob, you can lead one, Jake the other," Alison said, taking charge as they all gathered around the bins of overalls and helmets at the paintball center.

What the hell she was doing here, Sass wondered, playing games with the people she'd come to fight? They'd all come out together in the van after dropping Jacob off with a babysitter, picking up the boys and then stopping for this Alison woman, who'd checked Sass out as if she were a bug from under some stone.

"I'll take Moana," said Jake.

"Oi, you can't choose my wife like that," Rob protested.

"Just have. Whatcha going to do about it?"

"Steal Sass," Rob replied. "All Americans were born knowing how to shoot a gun, right?"

"Does a water pistol count?" she asked.

"Good enough." He put on a Darth Vader voice. "Come over here to the dark side, my child."

"And I'll be on Jake's team," Alison said quickly, "to stop him from getting too bossy."

"That's not fair," Brad pointed out. "You're the two best shots."

"Well, you're the third best, so we'll have you," Rob said. "Besides, it's all in the strategy. With Sass's brain and mine, they stand no chance."

"Yeah, yeah! Talk is cheap, brother. I'll take Pete. You can have both twins."

Moana was busy sorting gear. "Here, Sass, try these on for size."

She caught the overalls Moana threw to her. They were paint-stained, damp and very grubby. She looked ruefully down at her own clothing before wriggling into them.

"You'll need this, as well," Jake said, handing her a helmet. His overalls were likewise grimy, but though baggy on the backside, they were taut across his shoulders. He looked like a raffish action hero.

Sass jammed the helmet down over her French roll. It felt clammy.

"Team photos," Alison cried, squeezing in next to Jake. "You go over there, Sass, with your team."

"Yup, let's get a photo of the team that's going to win," Rob said, gathering his band about him and flinging a friendly arm around Sass's shoulders as the paintball owner dutifully took photos on Alison's camera.

"Not with an aim like yours you won't," Jake retorted. "I've seen you miss entire trees."

"Only because they moved. Keep talking it up, little brother, doesn't bother me."

Sass couldn't help smiling at the fraternal rivalry. She was reminded of her own brothers when they'd been young and full of cheek—before everything had gone wrong.

"Are you ready, Sass? Good, then we'll head out to the battlefield, where we get our weapons."

With a nod, she began following Rob and the rest of her team down the hill. The sun blazed; the overalls were hot and snagged on bushes as she passed. If she was in New York right now she could be dropping into an art gallery, meeting friends for coffee. Oh, who was she kidding? If she wasn't at work, she'd be at home, prepping for some case or other, dressed in sweats. For kicks she'd do a half hour on the treadmill and catch a late-night movie on TV.

Here she was hot as hell and desperately trying not to think of the sweaty head that had previously inhabited her helmet. But at the same time she felt a strange stirring in her blood.

It's only a game, she told herself, but a primitive part of her came to life. Ahead she could see her enemy. Topping everyone by several inches, his sun-bleached hair glinting in the light, Jake moved light-footed as an Apache. Alison, small and muscular beside him, talked urgently in a low voice, no doubt planning their attack.

Sass looked about her. The bushy hills and valleys stretched dizzyingly to the horizon in front, and behind the sea glinted in the afternoon sun. She wished she could sit and take it all in. Instead what she was going to get, she was pretty sure, was a running battle with Alison, who for some reason had really taken a dislike to her.

"Looking forward to this?" Brad was at her elbow.

"Sort of," Sass said. "It's not really my kinda thing."

"Don't worry, it doesn't hurt that much when you get shot—unless it's on the shin or the ribs," he added.

"That's a relief. I'll stay kneeling, with my elbows tucked in at my sides then."

Brad grinned, refusing to believe anyone could be that fainthearted, and continued with his advice. "Just shoot at anything that moves. Don't pause, keep going no matter what."

"Right."

"And whatever you do, don't let Jake get you in his line of fire. He never misses."

"Gotcha."

That mildly titillating thrill was replaced with dread. She was a city girl, for chrissakes!

Halfway down the steep hill they came upon a large tent, where both teams were armed, two flags given out and the rules explained. "One fort is in the gully, the other on top of the hill."

"We'll take the top of the hill," Alison declared.

At exactly the same time Jake said, "We'll take the gully."

They looked at each other, then she shrugged. "Yeah, okay. We'll take the gully. We can fight uphill."

"That's the spirit," Rob encouraged.

The teams split up.

"See you in my sights, honey," Moana called out.

"Always ready to draw your fire," her husband responded.

Sass wished she had someone she could joke with. *Going into battle without a friend in the world,* she thought ironically. And a little wistfully.

"Take care, America," Jake called out. "You may never have been invaded, but there's always a first."

"Ain't seen no threats so far, boy," she replied in her broadest Southern drawl.

Jake laughed and bounded away down the hillside with the joyousness of the superfit. Alison followed, after eyeballing Sass. The two were honestly looking forward to this.

"Now, Sass, do you want to guard the fort or go capture the flag?" Rob asked.

The devil and the deep blue sea. But not for nothing had one of Sass's great-great-great-granddaddies been a hero in the Civil War. "I'll join the invading forces," she said.

"Thatta girl!" Rob exclaimed. "With those legs, you should be fast." Quickly, he gave the boys their positions, and was outlining a few tactics when the whistle blew.

"That's us. Good luck, team." Rob jumped down a small gully and disappeared into the bush, crouching as he ran. Brad let out a warrior whoop and disappeared on the other side. Somehow Mark and Mike melted into the shadows, and suddenly Sass felt alone, exposed on the sunbaked hillside. She squatted down, feeling also very foolish.

"Dumb game," she muttered, but nevertheless began making her way down the hillside, dodging from tree to bush in the best Western fashion. The gun was heavy, but also reassuring. Something moved and she shot.

"Not me!" Brad whispered furiously.

"Sorry," she stage-whispered back. Oh, God, it was beginning to look like a very long afternoon.

The air erupted into stuttering gunfire and there was a frustrated cry.

"Damn, shot already!" Moana said as she emerged from the shadows, hands and gun in the air, making her way back to the tent, where she had to wait three minutes. "Just you wait for tonight, Rob Finlayson. There'll be no mercy for shooting your beloved wife."

"Can't wait." His disembodied voice floated back.

The leaves around Sass hissed and danced, and she realized someone was shooting at her. She dived, but even as she hit the ground, pain ricocheted up her arm from her elbow, where she'd been hit, and she yelped.

"Yes!" said a woman. Alison. Of course.

The next twenty minutes were hard-fought as paintballs whizzed in all directions. The enemy seemed to be all around her in the bushes and Sass shot indiscriminately, ducking, weaving and diving across the hillside. The sun blazed down as she sweated under the overalls, her helmet clammier than ever. The visor was claustrophobic and made the world seem vaguely unreal. Her Italian loafers slithered and slipped on the rough ground.

Disorientated, she rounded a small bluff, and instantly everything seemed to grow still. The shots and cries of battle receded and she could even hear a bird in one of the trees. Sighing with relief, she took off the helmet and shook her hair free of the sweaty French roll. The craving for a cigarette, which had begun in the van coming out, was now insistent. She glanced around. There was no one here. Settling her back against a tree, Sass lit up and inhaled deeply as she put the box on the ground beside her. Oh my, but that was good. Sanity seeped back into her bones and she closed her eyes, the sun warm on her lids. Drowsily, she drew on her cigarette. There was nothing—nothing—to equal the joy of a cigarette.

The box beside her bucked and she jumped, staring down in bewilderment. Red paint leaked through the destroyed cardboard cigarette box. With a furious cry, Sass whipped around, to see Jake laughing behind her.

"Thought you'd escape, did you? Told you, smoking isn't allowed."

Her peace violated, Sass snatched up her gun and sent a volley of paintballs at her tormentor. There was satisfaction in seeing him dive for the cover of nearby bushes. He gave a small cry, then Sass heard the sickening sound of his body falling, tearing out bushes and breaking branches as he went. Throwing her rifle to one side, she ran to where he had dived. The bushes had screened a small cliff face, not high, but very steep, and Jake lay motionless on a narrow shelf near the bottom. With an exclamation, Sass slithered down, gripping bushes and tufts of grass to slow her descent. How on earth would it look in New York if they discovered she'd managed to eliminate one of their chief protagonists in armed combat?

Once on the ledge, she crouched beside Jake and whipped off his helmet to check his breathing.

His eyes opened. "Are you going to give me the kiss of life?" He sounded breathless, but there was no sign of injury. There was, however, teasing laughter in those green eyes.

"You rat!" Relieved, Sass thumped him hard on his chest, causing him to jackknife. "I was worried, and you played dead on purpose!"

"I didn't," he protested. "I was just getting my breath back when you came and ripped off my helmet."

"Well, I can see you're fine," she said, trying to reclaim her dignity in this ridiculous situation. She rose, intending to climb back up to her gun, but her stupid pumps skated on the loose earth and this time it was she who slipped. Jake made a grab for her but it was too late, and they both fell off the ledge, rolling in a tangle down the last part of the slope and landing with a whump at the bottom, Jake plastered on top of her.

For a second both were too taken aback to move, then he pushed himself up on his arms, his weight still pinning her. “Are you okay?”

“Yeah, I think so.”

She knew she ought to get him off her, but it was as though the scene had been put on pause. Looking into his face, she saw his concern being replaced by something else. The sun behind his head lit his tousled mop like a halo, but there was nothing saintly about the catch in his breath. She felt the thud of her heart, heard the rasping of a cicada close to her left ear. The sun was hot on her shins, but her face was protected by Jake’s shadow. She could smell his sweat and the dust that coated them both. There was also a faint scent from one of the bushes they had crushed.

His weight bore down on her and—no, she was not going to think how wonderful it felt. Slowly his face came down to hers, and she felt his breath on her cheek. She lay absolutely still. It seemed an eternity before his lips reached hers in a soft kiss. Sass closed her eyes and almost dreamily parted her lips. The kiss deepened and the world dissolved around her as his weight, his mouth on hers, invaded all her senses. Then she pushed up, twisting with her hips, and he relaxed, allowing her to roll him so that now she lay on top. Burying her fingers in his hair, she took her turn exploring his mouth, surrendering to glorious, mindless, animal instincts. His hands tightened across her back, and as her hips pressed against his, she became aware of his arousal. Somehow this fact got through to her stupid brain.

This was all wrong.

With a wrench that was almost physically painful she pulled back and slipped sideways off his body. He gave a muffled protest and his hands caught at her, then let her go. She wasn't sure whether this was out of respect for her wishes or because he, too, was coming to his senses. She was surprised that not knowing bothered her.

"We shouldn't have done that," she said.

"No." He cleared his throat and blinked. The sun must've blinded him because he shut his eyes again. "Sorry."

"It must be the heat or the adrenaline or something. You don't have to apologize."

"Not for kissing you. For startling you in the first place." He smiled, eyes still closed. "Mind you, if I'd known it would provoke such a response, I'd have done it sooner."

Her heart tripped but she said, "We ought to be getting back to the game."

"Yeah." He rolled over and sat up, shaking his

head. "Pity we aren't allowed to take prisoners." He rose and put out his hand to pull her up, too.

"Why? Who'd be the prisoner, you or me?" Sass asked as she came to her feet, her head not very much lower than his.

"Good question. I'd be happy either way."

"This doesn't change anything," she said. He looked down at her and she looked steadily back at him. "It shouldn't have happened. I'd appreciate it if you would forget what just took place." She'd never had her brain say one thing and her treacherous senses something quite different.

He hesitated, eyes narrowed and searching her face. "Would you? Well, if that's how you want to play it…"

"I don't mix business with other stuff."

He nodded. "*Other stuff* would certainly complicate matters." His expression and tone had both hardened.

She stuck out her hand as though to bring some professionalism into this absurd moment. "Then we are agreed. This incident never happened."

"Agreed," he said, taking her hand. But instead of shaking it, he turned it over to kiss her pulse, which, unforgivably, skipped. "It's forgotten already." Swinging his helmet up in one hand and his gun with the other, Jake disappeared into the bush.

Sass was left staring at the trees that had closed

about him. Why did she feel desolate? She held her wrist. Had that been a caress or a challenge? One thing she knew for sure, from now on she'd be keeping a close eye on him—and herself.

CHAPTER FIVE

JAKE BARELY SAW SASS the following day. He took the boys to a regional competition, and though he made a rather ungracious offer to include her, she declined, saying she'd rather read the books Rob had lent her. They'd returned home late and saw no sign of her other than the kitchen looking unusually clean and tidy. She must have accepted his invitation to help herself to whatever she fancied. Funny how even when not seeing her, he could somehow sense her presence all around him.

On Monday morning, Jake dropped her off in Whangarimu to do some shopping, while he met Rob and Moana for coffee at a waterfront café. He tried to relax, but when a text message from Sass arrived, his temper, uncertain all morning, ignited.

"Of all the ridiculous—where the hell does she think she is?"

"What's up?" Rob asked.

"It's from Miss Pain-in-the. She doesn't want

a lift home, says she'll find her own way back." His voice was loaded with sarcasm.

"How?"

"She doesn't say. She probably thinks she can catch the subway or some daft notion. If she takes a taxi, it'll cost her a fortune."

"Text her and find out what she's planning to do," Moana suggested.

The answer winged back.

"Oh my God, she's rented a car! Now I'll find her in a ditch somewhere after driving on the wrong side of the road. What the hell is she trying to prove?"

Moana shrugged. "I don't see what the big deal is. She only wants a bit of independence."

"She's doing it," said Jake, "to get at me."

"Oh, come on. Hiring a car is not a personal insult." Rob stirred sugar into his coffee. "I don't see why you're getting so het up about it."

"It's a symbol," said Jake darkly.

Moana laughed at this, tossing her hair back over her shoulders as she rocked the pram where six-month-old Jacob lay sleeping. "Of what? I don't get what's going on between you two. I thought the paintball was supposed to improve international relations, but you were both even frostier on the way home than on the way out. What's Sass done to rile you so much?"

Rob cocked an eyebrow. "Anything happen at paintball that we should know about?"

Jake forced a short laugh. "C'mon, you were there. Where was the opportunity for anything?"

Rob's eyes narrowed. "Is that an evasion?"

He was rescued from interrogation by Jacob, who woke at that moment with a yell. Jake never lied to Rob, but somehow he couldn't begin to say what had happened out there. He'd lost his mind temporarily—it was the only explanation. As for the American, he must surely have imagined that momentary, unbridled passion. It couldn't really be lurking under her impenetrable calm. Jake wasn't used to being given the brush-off, and he was most certainly not used to caring on the rare occasion he was. Furthermore, he *was* used to sleeping soundly every night, so his resentment had been compounded when, at three in the morning, he'd found himself awake, libido in knots, wondering what the hell he was trying to prove with this stupid celibacy kick, anyway.

Sass, of course, had been as cool and as annoyingly imperturbable as ever during the drive into town earlier. She'd said she wanted to look around, and Jake had been glad to drop her off and leave her to her own devices for a few hours. The fact that the whole of Whangarimu shopping center could be done in under an hour had given him a small flash of malicious satisfaction. He'd thought once she discovered how hicksville they really were, she'd be ready to catch the next flight out. Instead, it seemed she was already finding her feet, taking control.

With Jacob still screaming, Rob and Moana said hasty farewells and, freed from the necessity of picking Sass up, Jake decided to drop into the local polytechnic. He survived financially by taking a series of temporary jobs such as farm work and teaching the conservation course part-time. This last job was proving more challenging than he'd thought. Who'd have ever guessed teachers put so much time and thought into their classes? Still, he loved the subject and his students, but the copious paperwork that went with the territory proved to be his bête noire. He was struggling with mounds of neglected filing when Colin popped his head around the door of Jake's tiny office.

"Ah, there you are. Heard rustlings and thought it might be rats. Then I heard the swearing."

Jake looked up at his colleague from the pile he'd just knocked off the desk. "Can't believe how much junk accumulates in such a short time. Good thing I'm only part-time. If I were full-time, I'd be buried alive under avalanches of this crap."

Colin stepped over another teetering pile and perched on a chair after removing yet more papers. His habitual good humor was intact. But beneath his thinning, sandy hair, his pale blue eyes were considerably sharper than his mild manner suggested. "Systems, that's what you need."

Jake grimaced. "Yeah, I know. I just seem biologically programmed to be incapable of following any."

Colin looked from Jake's biceps to his own thin, freckled arms. "I haven't heard your female students complain about your biological programming."

"It doesn't impress management, however."

Colin shook his head. "That's not what I've heard. Numbers enrolling in conservation have rocketed—and not just girls. Rumor has it you've turned down offers for a full-time contract twice. Why's that? I thought you were skint."

Jake laughed as he leaned back and swung on his computer chair. "Yeah, well, it's true I could do with the money but—" he hesitated "—full-time is a real commitment."

Colin surveyed him. "More fun to be had on the surfing circuit?"

"Nah, I've been there, done that. Teaching is fun and I really enjoy it. It's just—" Again Jake broke off, not sure himself what his objections were. "It just seems so final." He knew that sounded lame, the minute the words were out. He wasn't surprised when Colin shook his head.

"Listen to you. You sound like a kid of eighteen instead of a man in his thirties. It's got to happen sooner or later. You can't float on the surface of life forever. You need to put down some roots, mate."

Jake pulled a face. "Think I've been on the road too many years to settle down now."

"No desire for a wife and a home one day?" Colin eyed him curiously.

"Yeah, I'd like them someday—just not now."

"Spoken like a true commitment-phobe."

"Commitment-phobe?" Jake feigned outrage. "In case you hadn't noticed, I'm up to my bloody neck in commitments at the present."

Colin scratched his chin, a gesture he did when pondering an interesting phenomenon in the science lab. "Hmm, but they're all short-term, aren't they. The boys are only with you until the championships, the book has its deadline and as for the resort, well, that's going to be settled sooner or later. Then what? Will you stay on and see how things go for the tern?"

His tone was dispassionate; he was simply analyzing the situation from an objective point of view. But it left Jake feeling disconcerted, even a little defensive.

"I haven't planned that far ahead," he said with a shrug.

Colin leaned back and folded his arms. "You know what your problem is?"

"No, and I don't want to hear it from you, either."

His colleague smiled but continued, unperturbed. "You're still searching for the next best thing—the perfect wave. But a surfer like you should know there's no such thing. You've got to take what's in front of you."

"What's in front of me," said Jake, making a sweeping gesture, "is this bloody nightmare, and the next best thing I need is a shredder. Is there one I can use?"

Colin laughed as he got to his feet. "Yeah, there's one in the admin block. Okay, champ, have it your way. See you in a couple of weeks."

THE OLDER MAN'S WORDS stayed with Jake, however, and as he drove home, his thoughts were bleak. It wasn't only his desk that was a mess, his whole life needed systems. He was already past one deadline for the book he was writing on the fairy tern. How could he tell the publishers he'd stalled with it? All his energies, he told himself, were being used up in the battle to keep the invading Americans at bay. How could a man work when his home was threatened?

Damn Rob for saddling him with the woman. It just added to Jake's responsibilities, this need to make her fall in love with Aroha Bay. If she had eyes in her head, she'd see for herself what a travesty a holiday resort would be in such a place. The last thing in the world he needed right now was to play host to some insufferable hotshot.

As for the boys…he'd bitten off more than he could chew there. It had been a great idea at the time—just like the book had been—but the reality was considerably more difficult than he'd expected. He'd had some cool idea that it would be like a surf camp and that as long as they were focused on surfing, the rest of their lives would sort out. Instead, the house was constantly a wreck and the boys seemed to need feeding every minute of the day.

What's more, he had a feeling that even though it was still early in the school year, they were probably not doing as well as they should. The boys never seemed to do any homework, but Jake didn't want to harp on about assignments and tests. God, he'd sound like his old man, and Brad was always squaring up against him as it was. What was up with the kid? He pretended it was all a joke, but he never missed an opportunity to make a dig at Jake, to defy his authority.

Jake still believed that Aroha Bay was what the

boys needed, but Janet, their social worker, seemed unconvinced a single male was the best guardian for them. She'd been clearly unimpressed by the state of the house the last visit, and had said she'd drop by again soon. Despite her smile, it had sounded like a threat, and he knew she'd be along any day now. He really needed to clean ASAP, stock the fridge with fresh salad, that sort of thing. That's what she'd be looking for. He could lose the boys otherwise. As he could lose the battle for Aroha Bay and the fairy tern.

Jake hated the mere thought of losing.

As he swung down the driveway to the house, his stress levels mounted. What he really craved was a surf but instead he'd have to cook dinner and sort through some of the bills that were cluttering the table. He probably also ought to entertain the American, though how, he couldn't imagine. Well, he could. But that image was sharply repressed.

The first thing he saw, sitting jauntily next to the sleep-out, was the car. A red convertible. Bloody typical! He might have guessed she'd get something like that. He was amazed the boys weren't all standing around it, tongues hanging out and begging for rides. Brad would be itching to drive. Oh, man, yet another battle Jake simply didn't need. He pulled up next to the convertible and jumped out, slamming his door. There was no sign of Sass, but music was pounding out of the house. No guesses where the boys were, then. Delicious smells wafted across the grass. Cooking? No one in the house *cooked.* Jake bounded up the deck steps, then stopped short in the doorway. For a second he thought he must have the wrong house. The wrong boys.

"Hi, Jake," Paul said with one of his shy, sidelong looks that substituted as a smile. He was polishing the glass of the bay window.

"Did you bring a game home?" Mike asked. He was sitting cross-legged on the floor, putting all the loose DVDs and Xbox games into the right cases and stacking them.

"We were hoping you might pick up that new racing one," Mark added from his perch on top of the sofa, where he was cleaning the cobwebs from the corners.

"Oh, you're home," Brad said as he passed through the lounge, lugging a vacuum cleaner. "Did you see the car? Isn't she a little beauty?"

"What the hell is going on?" Jake roared.

The boys all paused.

"We're cleaning," said Brad in a "well, duh" tone.

"But you guys don't clean. You are the worst pigs I've ever met. If I tell you to put something away, you act like I'm the most unreasonable brute in the world."

Brad grinned. "Ah, but that's because you're a crap cook."

Jake shot him a look.

"Sass said she'd make Mexican if we cleaned the house. It's got to be spotless. She's an amazing cook," one of the twins elaborated.

"How do you know?"

"She made us Texan burgers when we came back from school this afternoon. Said her brothers were always starving when they were our age. You've never tasted anything like these burgers. Then she offered us a deal. She'll cook while she stays here so long as we keep the place clean."

Jake couldn't begin to untangle his thoughts and feelings on hearing that. Of all the managing, bossy, conniving… As for the boys, what a bunch of mercenary turncoats. At the same time, something did smell fantastic.

"Where is she?"

"In the kitchen."

Jake went through and there, sure enough, was Sass stirring a pot. She was humming, her back to him, and looking like every man's fantasy in a short denim skirt and a clinging white tee. Her blond hair was pulled up in a ponytail and a big

Texan belt was slung around her slender hips. She didn't hear him come in and he took a minute to look around the kitchen. Everything had been scrubbed, polished and put away. Every surface gleamed. He didn't know that things on the stove could smell so good, either. He was not, however, so easily bought as the boys.

"What the *hell* is that?"

Sass turned. "Oh, you're back." It was a statement of fact, not a welcome. "That's an espresso machine."

"I can see that. Where did it come from?"

"A shop called Brisket or something like that."

"Briscoes. What's it doing here? I don't drink coffee."

"But I do."

"You're only here for a week."

She leaned against the counter and folded her arms across her chest, as calm and cool as ever, despite the heat of the kitchen.

"Trust me, you don't want to be around if I don't get my daily caffeine fix. I'll leave it for your next guests. How're the boys doing? Dinner's nearly ready."

"I guess I should thank you." He didn't feel in the slightest bit grateful.

"No need, I didn't do it to please you. Would you like to go and wash up? I'm serving in ten."

INSTEAD OF EATING with plates on their laps, as was their custom, they sat at the cleared, cleaned table. When Jake came through, the boys were already there, looking surprisingly civilized and decidedly hungry.

"Flowers?" he said, with a nod to the vase of yellow roses. "A bit of a waste on five blokes, isn't it?"

Sass blushed, but before she could reply Paul said softly, "My mum used to put flowers on the table."

Jake and the other boys stared at him. He never spoke about his mother. She'd died eighteen months earlier.

"Did she?" The annoyance on Sass's face disappeared and she smiled at Paul. She began handing out plates for the boys to help themselves. Jake saw from her eyes that she'd registered Paul's use of the past tense, but her voice was light when she asked, "Did she enjoy gardening?"

Paul gave her a hesitant smile. "Couldn't get her out of it—especially in summer."

"I bet. A garden's the one thing I'd really like in New York."

Jake was impressed, despite himself. Paul wasn't one to volunteer information, and he almost never smiled. There was something in Sass's manner that the boys were instinctively turning to. It wasn't that she was motherly—more like a big sister. She must have been great with her own brothers.

"It looks good," he said, prepared to have a truce with a person who could tame this brood.

Brad grinned. "It tastes even better. Oh, and you owe Sass three hundred and forty-eight bucks."

"What?"

Sass threw Brad a reproving look. "I told you not to mention it. It's not a big deal."

"What three hundred dollars?" Jake demanded.

"For the electricity," Brad continued, ignoring Sass. "They cut the power off this morning."

"Bastards!" Jake was mortified that Sass should see he wasn't coping.

"We found the bills in the pile of shit over there—" Brad waved toward the overflowing in-tray on top of the piano "—and Sass rang and paid over the phone with her credit card. Man," he continued admiringly, "you should have heard the way she sweet-talked the guy into reconnecting us immediately. Tell you what, you're going to have a fight on your hands if Sass decides against you guys."

"Can it, motormouth." Sass glared at him, then looked at Jake. "It's not an issue. I'd have been paying to stay in a hotel. Consider this my contribution to staying here, instead."

"Thank you," said Jake stiffly, "but I won't hear of you paying my bills."

They locked eyes. Sass's head tilted before she shrugged and smiled. That polite smile of hers, not the real one she kept for the boys, for Rob and Moana—for everyone except him. "Sure, pay me back whenever."

She then turned the conversation to surfing, a guaranteed way to get the boys talking, leaving Jake to enjoy his Pyrrhic victory. In silence he devoured his meal. It was as good as it smelled but he wished it had been burned or undercooked or something. She made him feel so damned incompetent. The dining room, like the kitchen, had been transformed. She must have had the boys working like galley slaves all afternoon. Not that it would last long. Jake pulled these ungracious thoughts up short. Here he was with a clean house, electricity and dinner, and she wasn't even looking for his gratitude. She'd done it purely to suit herself. He ought to enjoy it. He ought to, but he couldn't shake the feeling that she was invading every facet of his life. Typical American, the original invader.

The phone rang and he left the table to answer it.

"Hi, it's Moana. I'm just phoning to remind you about the party on Saturday night."

He swore.

"I knew you'd forget! Look, Rob and I think it would be nice to invite Sass along, too."

"She wouldn't be interested."

"Ask her."

"You ask her," he said gracelessly.

"Oh, Jake." Moana sighed. He could picture her shaking her head. "Put her on the line then."

Jake called out to Sass, "Moana wants a word."

As he took his place again at the table he could hear her soft American intonations that conjured visions of large white Southern mansions with those mile-long, tree-lined drives that were always in movies.

"You're inviting me out? That's so sweet of you, I'd love to come." She listened. "Yeah, it's a cute little red car… A bit strange getting used to driving on the other side of the road… No, he hasn't mentioned it… We're having dinner right now…" She laughed. "No, I cooked… Yes, I can cook! What do you think I am?" She laughed again. Jake knew Moana was liking her more and more. Was this interloper going to bewitch everyone? Couldn't they *see?* "Yeah, see you tomorrow night at the meeting… The boys' parents will be there? Well, I'll look forward to it. Bye for now."

She hung up and returned to the table.

"So I get to meet your folks tomorrow night."

"You're going to meet Jake's dad?" Brad laughed. "That'll be a trip for both of you."

Great, Jake thought, *just great.*

But, as usual with life, the moment he thought things couldn't get any worse, there was a knock at the door. He went through to the lounge and his heart plummeted. Through the glass doors he could see Janet's small, square frame topped with frizzy hair and hazel eyes that saw far too much. He'd known this moment would come, but he was in no way ready for it. Drawing in a deep breath he forced a smile as he threw open the door. "Janet! Great to see you."

CHAPTER SIX

JANET SMILED. "I hope this isn't an inconvenient time to call."

Her last visit had really caught him on the hop. He'd seen her nose wrinkle at the mess spread across the floor, the unmade beds, the remains of baked beans, fried eggs and toast in the kitchen.

"Not at all. Perfect timing, in fact. We're all here. Come on in." His voice had all the assurance he lacked.

She stepped into the lounge and looked around, astonished. "What an improvement. Well done. To be honest, I wasn't sure you'd ever be able to get the place sorted out."

"Yeah, it looked terrible, but it was all superficial. Nothing that couldn't be taken care of in an afternoon." Well, that last sentence was true, at any rate. "Come on through and see the boys. We're having dinner. Will you join us?"

"Oh, no, this is just a quick visit, thanks. It smells delicious, but I'm having dinner at a friend's—" She broke off. Jake couldn't blame her. Reentering the dining room he was struck by how homey everything looked—the glossy tabletop, the steaming bowls, the boys' blissful faces and yes, dammit, even the flowers. Janet's surprise was compounded, however, by Sass's presence. She stood staring, a small frown between her eyebrows that did not smooth out as Sass rose and held out her hand.

"Hi, I'm Sass Walker."

As they shook hands, Jake explained. "Sass is from Paradise Resorts."

"Oh, I see." Clearly, Janet did not. She turned back to him. "I thought you were petitioning against it."

"I am. Sass is in New Zealand to fight the petition."

"Here to find an amicable solution," Sass countered smoothly. "Jake and the boys are kindly letting me stay in their sleep-out."

She was quick, Jake had to admit. She'd immediately seen Janet speculating as to their relationship, and was making it quite clear where she slept.

Janet nodded. "I see," she repeated, but this time in a different tone. Then she turned her attention to the boys. "Hello, everyone."

"Hi, Janet," they chorused. Then, to both Janet's and Jake's amazement, Brad rose, looking sheepish, followed by the others. Jake shot a look at Sass, standing just behind Janet, and caught her tiny nod of approval to the boys. She must have communicated some need for manners to Brad with a jerk of her head. But it worked. Janet was taken aback but impressed.

"Do sit," she said with a laugh. "I don't want to disturb your dinner. I'll catch up with you individually after school one day next week. Is that okay?"

They all smiled with a quick raise of their eyebrows, which, in Kiwi teenage malespeak, served as affirmation, before falling on their food again.

"I must say," said the social worker, gazing around, "the house looks amazing."

She glanced speculatively at Sass. Jake held his breath. Sass gave her Southern-girl-I'm-so-charmed-by-everything smile.

"Doesn't it," she agreed. "When I first arrived, I couldn't believe the way these guys looked after the place."

She was better than good. She was downright devious. But now that he knew she was, for the moment, on his side, Jake could relax and enjoy the show.

"Have you been here long?"

"Only a few days."

"Mexican food, I see. Did you cook it?" The

question was tossed off, but Janet's eyes were steady. Sass held her gaze.

"Yes, Jake didn't want me to, of course. He's such a host, but I insisted. I was missing my kind of food and thought the boys might like it, too."

Jake could feel himself flush. He knew what a crap host he had been.

"Jake's so busy," Sass continued, her voice all molasses and summer breeze lilt, "yet he still does all the work for these boys. I've been telling them it's time they learned to cook some."

"It's true," Brad interjected. "She's going to teach us how to make American pancakes for breakfast tomorrow."

"Is she?" Janet nodded, then turned her sharp eyes back on Sass. "I can't believe how this place has been transformed."

A tiny frown of incomprehension formed between those deep blue eyes of Sass's. "Yeah? I've only been here a few days, of course." Her apologetic shrug clearly said she didn't know what Janet was talking about.

The social worker smiled. "Well, I won't keep you from your dinner. I would hate the food to get cold. Delighted to see everything's going well. Nice meeting you, Sass. We may bump into each other again."

"I sure hope so," she said.

Janet bade farewell to the boys and Jake saw her back to her car. He noticed her glance at the sleep-out and was glad that Sass had, by chance, left a light on.

"I have to tell you, Jake," said Janet, stepping into the car while he held the door for her, "I had my doubts about your ability to cope after my last visit." She shook her head. "But I can see tonight that you've obviously got everything under control. My congratulations. If this continues, you can be sure of my support. You'll be going to the parent interviews at school tomorrow, I take it?"

He'd put it completely out of his mind, despising the whole idea. This wasn't what he'd thought he was buying into when Moana first suggested he mentor the kids, but Janet had told the boys to set up the interviews on her last visit. And now she was looking expectantly up at him.

"Of course." He smiled as he closed her door, but was glad that, in the dim light, she couldn't read how false it was. Damn, the meeting was tomorrow night and he'd also promised to help Mac up on the farm with building a fence. He'd just have to fit it all in somehow.

Janet wound down her window and stuck her head out. "That American. How long is she staying?"

"Just a few more days."

"She's very beautiful."

"I guess—in an American sort of way." His tone was dismissive.

Janet nodded and smiled again. "Make sure the boys don't all get crushes on her."

He laughed. "As if. None of us can think of anything but the coming surf comps."

Her last doubts seemingly reassured, the woman said goodbye. Jake stood, watching her taillights disappear, before going back into the house. The boys were buzzing. Even Paul was laughing.

"Did you see her face?"

"Man, Sass, you were great!"

"She honestly bought it."

"Jake!" Brad said. "Wasn't that cool!"

"Sass," he said, smiling ruefully as he took his seat, "I owe you big-time. The boys told you she was their social worker, I gather."

She shook her head. "They didn't need to. I could tell right off. I guess social workers the world over must have the same look about them."

He stopped with his fork halfway to his mouth. "You've met a few in your time, then? Did you used to work in juvenile law?"

"No, but I saw a lot when I was growing up."

Jake was glad when Mike asked the next question. "How come? I thought you were from some posh home."

This made Sass laugh. "No. I grew up in a trailer park."

"No way!" Brad expressed everyone's disbelief. "You have way too much style."

"That's kind of you to say, but no, when I was your age, I lived in a trailer." She hesitated the merest fraction, but Jake could see she was weighing how much to say. Then, with the tiniest shrug, she continued. "My dad just up and went one day, leaving behind a large number of debts. My mom had to sell the house to pay them off and we moved into a trailer. So yeah, I knew all about social workers long before I studied law."

She let her words sink in and the boys nodded, accepting her as one of them. Watching this, Jake felt some of his antipathy toward the woman dissolving. He'd assumed she'd been born some Southern belle in a *Dallas* type family with J.R. as her father.

Somewhat awkwardly, he said, "Well, I'm grateful." She slanted him a skeptical look and he added, "No, really. I'm indebted to you."

This time she smiled back—her real smile. "I didn't do *anything*. I just told the truth."

This made all the boys fall about laughing.

"Man, I've got to learn to tell the truth like that to teachers," Brad said.

"After tonight," Jake told her, "I'm going to tread more carefully than ever."

She nodded and her coolness returned. "I'm not your enemy, Jake. I'm only here to examine the situation and try to make an impartial decision."

"I can't be impartial. I've too much at stake." He was trying to tell her that despite everything, they couldn't be friends. It wasn't that simple. Suddenly, inappropriately, he remembered their kiss. He could almost feel her lips on his.

"We all have," she said.

Her tone was light, noncommittal and before he had a chance to speak, she changed the subject. "So what's the deal here? Why is Janet checking up on you like this?"

"We're bad and Jake's useless," Brad interjected.

Jake opened his mouth to protest, but laughed instead. "I guess that sums it up. Not quite, of course. They've all got surfing talent and they've all run into trouble." He paused, but the expected question didn't come. He grudgingly liked that. Most people couldn't wait to hear what sort of misdemeanors the boys had been involved in.

"We're called 'youth at risk,'" Mark added cheerfully.

Sass smiled. "One group of bad asses?"

The boys exchanged glances. They liked that. "Yeah," Paul said.

"There are all sorts of schemes going in New Zealand at present to help this sort," Jake explained. "The fence at the top instead of the ambulance at the bottom."

Sass nodded. "Sure, we have programs like that in the States."

"So you're familiar with this sort of thing—boot camps and outward-bound courses. Moana's brilliant idea was to have a surf camp, the boys living out here and training for the national competitions in a few months."

"I see," said Sass, assessing him. He felt himself grow red. Deep down he knew Janet's reservations about him were justified. The thought stung. But Sass surprised him. "Y'all don't know how lucky you are to have Jake."

Brad guffawed, but Sass fixed him with a look. "I mean it. I wish somebody had stepped in with my brothers."

"Why? Did they get into trouble?" Paul asked shyly.

Again Sass hesitated. Then, putting whatever reservations she might have to one side, she said, "Yeah. Adam, my baby brother, ended up being a father when he wasn't much older than you guys." That made Brad wince, Jake was pleased to note. "He made his living as a stunt rider. Wouldn't listen to anyone—more guts than brains.

Crashed doing a damned stupid act everyone told him was crazy, and spent a year in hospital with a broken back, among other things."

"Shit," said Mike, exchanging glances with his twin. They both pushed the limits constantly with their skateboards.

"Yeah. His wife took off with their kid, too. He hasn't seen his daughter in years. He won't talk about it, but I can tell it eats him up."

The boys, however, didn't care about losing some kid. "What about the other one?"

Sass's eyes darkened. "Cole's in prison," she said softly.

"Ho," said Brad, awed. "What for?"

Jake saw her hands clench in her lap, but she kept her voice even. "Driving a getaway car. He was a hotshot driver and just saw it as a game—you know, taking on the establishment. He's not really criminal, not deep down." She met Brad's eyes and Jake knew she'd picked up that the boy was the one most at risk. "Both my brothers were dare-devils at heart, but they let it out in the wrong places. Life doesn't give us many chances. Jake's giving you guys a big fat one here. If you've got any brains at all, you'll be grabbing it with both hands."

Four heads swiveled in his direction and Jake looked down. He hadn't expected Sass's support.

The twins would follow him to hell and back, and Paul seemed to accept him—

"Yeah, whatever," said Brad.

Jake decided it was time to change the subject. "So, what about these parent interviews?"

There were groans from Brad and Paul. Mike and Mark looked smug. "Ours aren't for a few weeks," Mark said.

"What time do I need to be there?"

"It's a teachers-only day tomorrow, so we'll all be home," Brad reminded him, "but Paul and I made them for the afternoon. The first is at two."

Jake helped himself to more fajitas. "Jeez, it's going to be quite a day. I have to pop up to Mac's first."

"Great! Can you drop me and Paul in town?" Brad asked. "We want to see the new racing movie."

"Okay, we'll take the van."

"That heap of shit?" Brad shook his head. "It's got serious problems, man. It needs to be overhauled."

"Yeah, yeah. I'll get to it." Jake was irritated. He didn't have the time, money or interest to waste on a damned motor. Brad, a petrol-head, just didn't get that.

Sass cut through the gathering hostility. "And what will you twins do? Surf?"

"Yeah, if the waves are good," Mike said. "Xbox otherwise."

"Maybe I should come and watch," Sass suggested.

"Best come when Jake's out," Mark said. "He rocks."

"Yeah, you should see the video of him," Paul added. "Mike found it when we were cleaning up this afternoon."

"Video?" Sass raised her eyebrows.

"I should have thrown that thing out ages ago," Jake muttered. "It's nothing."

Never one to miss an opportunity to wind Jake up, Brad dived in. "No, you should watch it, Sass," he urged, "and see what Jake used to be like before he turned into such a *girl*."

"You were in a movie? Seriously?" Sass stared at him.

"It was a long time ago. No big deal."

"But it's so cool," Mark protested.

Sass leaned back in her chair, clearly enjoying his discomfiture. Any charitable thoughts he'd been entertaining about her in the past half hour disappeared.

"Don't be shy, Jake. I'd *love* to see it," she drawled. "All those boards and muscles."

"Trust me," he said through gritted teeth, "you'll be bored to tears within five minutes."

Ignoring him, Sass said to Mike, "Can you put the video on?"

"Sure can." He pushed his chair back. "I'll go set it up."

Jake got up and glowered at Brad and Mark, who were both grinning. "Well, if you're determined to drive our guest screaming mad, I refuse to have any part of it. I'm going to bed. Make sure you switch everything off before you turn in, okay?"

Sass looked guilelessly at him. Jake was not deceived. "You brought this on yourself by encouraging them. Don't say I didn't warn you."

SASS WATCHED as Jake turned on his heel and stalked out of the room. She knew he knew that had been an ungracious speech. Wow, they really had got to him. She felt a twinge of conscience. On the other hand it had been fun to see a cool surfer dude lose it like that. Seemed she'd just found his Achilles' heel. That could prove very useful, she thought as she followed the boys into the TV room.

Mike had pulled down a big screen that had been furled above the French doors, and it was now filled with images of huge blue waves. Loud surfing music blared from the speakers. Her quarry now gone, Sass settled into one of the battered armchairs with a sense of anticlimax. Fun over. Though she'd never admit it, she put surf movies of boys with bad haircuts and cheesy grins right up alongside televised golf as must-be-avoideds. Perhaps she could watch for a bit and then excuse herself, claiming exhaustion. A spring dug in under her backside and she had a craving for a cigarette. Dumb house rule.

Within minutes of the credits beginning to roll, however, Sass realized this was no corny Californian movie but a documentary, charting the history of big wave riders. These waves were enormous. Sass blinked. Did Jake…no, surely not. No way.

"I'll fast-forward to the bit with Jake," Mike said. "You don't want to sit through all these old guys talking about their youth. They were cool in their day, but—" he shrugged "—Jake's way out-surfed any of them."

Brad leaned back in his chair, in unconscious imitation of Jake. "Yeah, he's an old woman now, but man, he was something in those days. Out-gunned the lot."

The tumbling blur of waves, talking faces and men paddling out at double speed suddenly halted as Mike found the spot. "This is it! Jake in Hawaii."

Sass stared at Jake's face filling the screen. He was younger then, cockier, his hair more bleached and his face even more tanned. But unmistakably Jake. The man was exceptionally photogenic, with Hugh Jackman charisma. Alight with passion, his eyes looked greener than ever as he spoke about the almost spiritual joy that came with riding a big wave. Cut to Jake paddling up and up what the commentator referred to as a twenty-foot wave. Jake crested it as the lip began curling, then effortlessly spun, his arms digging deep, the muscles in his back rippling as he began the race to catch the next monster wave.

The helicopter with the camera rose to get out of the way as white spray lifted like a mist off the huge blue-black wave that picked Jake up and carried him like a piece of flotsam. Except he was not flotsam, he was fully in control. His powerful arms pulled him up to the lip, then with a jump he was standing and immediately sliding down the wave. The camera panned back to show him as a speck on the immense flank.

The microphone picked up the deafening roar as the white lip began chasing him down the face, threatening to bury him under tons of surging water. He swooped on, skimming and weaving, before plunging into the trough. Even though she *knew* he'd survived it, Sass was gripped with terror. His tiny figure wavered at the very bottom as the mountain of water finally caught and tumbled him, engulfing him in churning surf.

"You feel like a piece of lint in a washing machine," Jake's voice-over said. "All you can do is hold your breath and go with it until it stops. You have no idea which way is up and you hope like hell you don't find the reef. It'll shred you like you were an old newspaper. Then all of a sudden the weight lifts and you follow your leash up to where your board is floating."

The churning maelstrom cut back to a close-up of Jake grinning, eyes blazing, hair awry. "It's the biggest blast you can ever hope for," he said, looking out of the screen, seemingly straight into Sass's eyes. "Nothing else in life even comes close."

The documentary moved on, showing how Jet Skis enabled surfers to catch bigger and bigger waves in exotic locations. More dizzying drops, more tumbles into seething surf crashing against razor-edged rocks. And weaving through them all was Jake, larger than life but still only a splinter against the waves.

"Now for the greatest contest of big wave surfing," the commentary said, and Mike switched off the video.

"That's it. That's all that Jake was in."

"Not the competition?" Sass couldn't believe it. He'd been described as one of the hottest contenders.

"Nope," said Brad. "He didn't enter."

"How come?"

The boys exchanged glances and shrugged.

"He said it didn't seem important anymore," Mark said.

It didn't make sense, and clearly, the boys didn't think so, either.

"He dropped his balls," said Brad, and though the others demurred, no one came up with another explanation.

LATER, SASS LAY IN BED, one hand behind her head, staring out the open door to the night sky. She'd never seen stars as bright as here, but right now she wasn't thinking about them. Having just finished paging through surfing magazines the twins had dug out for her, she was wondering what made Jake tick. He'd been featured in many of them, an editor's dream with that jaw, those sun-streaked, untamed curls, those cool green eyes. He'd been one of the hottest properties on the surfing scene. So what had made him walk away from it all? He must have made a mint, so where the hell was all that money now? A surfer could dress in faded tees and threadbare shorts, but no guy with an ounce of testosterone would drive that van voluntarily.

His face was different, too. He'd seemed younger, yet most of the footage had been shot in the past couple of years. The diamond-hard cockiness she'd seen on the screen had been replaced by something more… She searched for a suitable word. Farseeing? Wiser? She couldn't quite put her finger on it.

Who was this guy? She'd already seen several sides to him—hostile SOB, teasing brother, surfer with a death wish and an ex-champion who got hotly embarrassed at reference to his success. Also, for those few moments, she'd glimpsed one very passionate lover. She sighed. *Know thy enemy.* How could she when she wasn't sure he knew himself? It would be real interesting to meet his folks, though.

Flipping onto her side, Sass tried to settle. Sleep took some time coming, however, and her dreams were a confusion of enormous tumbling waves, with herself, helpless as a rag doll, at the very bottom of them as a pair of cool green eyes watched.

CHAPTER SEVEN

SASS WAS INTO HER third mile the next morning when she heard Jake call, “Hey, Sass, are you around?” as he came up the steps.

Good of him to warn her he was approaching the curtainless glass doors, but still she was annoyed. She was just hitting her stride and didn’t want to be interrupted.

“Yeah,” she called out, trying not to lose pace.

He arrived at her open door and stopped abruptly. “What the hell is that?”

“A treadmill. I’ve rented it.”

“Why?” He looked genuinely amazed.

“To keep fit.” If she sounded brisk, it was because she had to conserve her breath.

“But why run in here when there’s all that?” He waved toward the beach and sea, splashed in early morning sunlight.

“It’s my routine.”

“Routine?”

"Yes, I run every day. The treadmill means I can keep track of my fitness."

He shook his head. "You are one sad lady." Even as he said that, though, his eyes were traveling over her body.

"Why?"

"To be indoors when you can be out—"

"Look, I work long hours, okay? I have to exercise when I can. Most of the time it's not safe to be out." She slowed her pace a little. Talking and running was hard work. He was really interfering with her regimen. At the same time, there was an easiness between them this morning that hadn't been there before. That social worker's visit seemed to have unlocked some of this dude's aggression. She didn't like to concede that her impression of him had modified, too.

"Yeah, but while you *are* here…never mind. I've come to see if you want to join us. The boys and I are going surfing."

She shook her head. "Sorry, but I've already got plans for this morning."

Was that annoyance that flitted across his face? It was gone so fast, she couldn't be sure.

"C'mon," he said, "you told Rob you'd get to know the place. See it as research."

He smiled, but she was damned if she'd succumb to his trademark surf charm like some teenage kid.

She needed to get to the library, get some background on Aroha Bay. But Jake was right, it would be useful to get the feel of the place. The library could wait until the afternoon.

"Okay, I'm nearly done, just another one and a half miles," she said. "I'll come over then."

He nodded, and if he felt triumphant, he hid it well. Today she was being treated to the perfect host. "Great. You'll enjoy the swim. The waves are beautiful this morning."

"I told you, I'm not into waves. I'm happy to watch, but I prefer swimming on the harbor side."

He propped a shoulder against the door frame. "New Zealand is wasted on you, Sass. You jog indoors, won't try the waves. I've never seen anyone so fainthearted."

Her stride didn't falter as she picked up the towel hanging over the bars of the treadmill and threw it at him. "Get outta here!"

He grinned as he caught it. "I dare you to go in the waves."

She fixed him with a look that was as stern as possible while loping along, sweat dripping into her eyes. She really, really didn't want to go into the waves. She'd be in his territory. However, there was an offer on the table, and as a lawyer, she couldn't resist.

"If I do, you've got to forfeit something."

"Like what?"

"Let me see the book you're writing."

He didn't even stop to consider it. "No *way.* It's nowhere near ready for publication."

"Brad tells me you've already missed one deadline."

"Brad's got a big mouth."

"You have to get used to people reading it. That's what books are for."

"Why are you interested?"

"Because I bet Brad you'd show it to me."

"Is that so?" She could tell he didn't know whether to be amused or annoyed. "Why?"

"He's promised to clean the oven if I can persuade you to let me see the book. It's a disgusting mess—the oven, I mean. I haven't seen the book yet."

"And?"

"And what?" It was hard to look innocent when she was becoming winded.

"There's got to be another reason."

"It's something you're shy about. He says no one's even had a glimpse of it yet. If you're pushing me out of my comfort zone, I'm going to push you out of yours, too."

Throwing back his head, Jake laughed. "I knew it! It's well masked, but you, Miss Pain-in-the, are a ball breaker."

She began running up a virtual incline. "So it's a deal?"

"I'll show you the first chapter."

"No. I want more."

"Three chapters?"

She could see this was really eating the guy. "Five chapters. That's my final offer. I can't settle for less or Brad won't buy it. I'm going to have a hard time convincing him, having sold out so low as it is."

Jake threw up his hands in defeat. "Okay, deal. But I'm quite sure you've got your clean oven, Ms. Walker. Brad doesn't stand a chance against you. And I don't want any helpful comments when I show the chapters to you. They're only in draft form, remember." Man, he was really insecure about this. He tried to cover up by adding, "Bloody Brad, I'll enjoy watching him sweat. Might go and put an extra layer of grease over the oven."

"Doesn't need it." She could only talk in short sentences now. "Go. I've a hill coming up."

He laughed again and hooked the towel over the rail. "Looking great," he murmured into her ear.

She stumbled and nearly lost her rhythm altogether. "Go on, get lost."

With a wink, he headed out the door.

A LITTLE LATER, in her swimsuit and a sarong, Sass crested the hill. She could see five figures out on the waves below her—two paddling out, three quite far out, sitting alert on boards. She could see the set of waves moving in.

They let the first wave go. The second was taken by two boys who swooped down the face, one tumbling in the whitewash as it reached the shore. She winced. The third wave was big and the remaining surfer took it. From his comparative size, she realized it was Jake. He swung into a crouch as he tipped over the edge of the wave and began weaving his way from the top to the bottom and back to the top again. One more long run brought him down its length and as it broke on the shoreline, he leaped lightly off into knee-deep water.

Jake had seen her watching, and waved. She returned the wave, making her way down the dunes toward him. His hair was swept off his face in a wet tangle; his biceps were taut as he held the board. The water sucked and pulled at his long legs. His green eyes were shining—the adrenaline, she guessed.

"That looked incredible."

"It was a fantastic wave," he agreed. "Want to come out?"

She shook her head. "I'd like to watch first."

"Okay." He cocked his head. "When you're ready, I'll leave the board and come out with you."

She felt a spurt of relief, but wasn't going to show weakness. "You really don't have to."

"I want to." He sounded genuine. "The waves aren't so big close to shore. I'll show you how to catch them."

"Mmm." She was unconvinced, but added a reluctant, "Okay."

She was already regretting her deal. It wasn't that she was afraid—exactly. She'd been in waves before, but she liked them small, predictable, with the ground never more than a couple of feet below her. What she *really* hated was the idea of being knocked down by the sea and feeling utterly powerless, yet there was no way she could ever express this fear to Jake.

He nodded and headed back into the water, throwing himself onto the board and paddling out with powerful strokes. Well, that explained the honed biceps and pecs. A wave broke and he ducked under the whitewash, popping up on the other side. He looked like a sea creature, she thought. A merman. She smiled at the foolish idea, but found it kind of sexy at the same time. She stretched out on her towel, propping up on her elbows to watch the action. Brad was next, running up exhilarated.

"The waves are fantastic. We've had some wicked rides."

Sass couldn't help laughing at his enthusiasm. "I've seen a couple. Y'all look great. Go on, get back to it."

He gave her a thumbs-up and ran into the water. The twins and Paul were too shy to come out to say hi, but waved to her as they circled around.

Sass had meant to study the beach and setting from a professional point of view, but she kept being sidetracked by the surfers in front of her. It was a beautiful sport, she discovered. The green-blue waves were almost transparent, the sky a brilliant blue. She didn't try differentiating between the figures on the boards, although Jake was always immediately identifiable, not only because of his height, but also because he rode the waves longer, more confidently. It was a joyous sport. There were whoops when one of the boys caught an exceptional wave. Laughter when one got knocked over. They sped down crests, then immediately paddled out again. It was exhausting just to watch them, but also mesmerizing. She lost track of time—she who charged for her work in ten minute increments and planned accordingly—and was surprised to see Jake making his way toward her.

"Ready for a swim?" he called.

She felt butterflies in her stomach. It was one

thing to watch these guys play like dolphins, it was another for her to go in. But she'd been dared. "Sure," she said, rising.

Was that approval she saw in his eyes before he lay his board down and undid his ankle strap? "Good," he said.

They walked to the water. "Have you swum in waves much?"

She shook her head. "Not really. I've only had one vacation by the sea and spent most of my time in the hotel pool."

"Then I'm the lucky one who'll introduce you to a new sort of heaven." Jake took her hand. "Come on, I won't let go."

"I don't need you to hold my hand," she said as they waded in. But as the water sucked and pulled at her feet, she appreciated the firm grip. The water was cold! It splashed up, making her gasp as they waded in past their knees.

"It's always best to dive in before it hits the crotch," Jake advised.

"I don't know…"

"I do. Count of three. Trust me. One. Two. Three."

Snatching a breath, she dived, keeping hold of Jake's hand. They surfaced together, laughing as she coughed, hair covering her face.

"Should have tied it up," she said, flipping it back off her forehead.

"It would be more practical," Jake agreed, "but now you look like a mermaid."

She shot him a withering look. No way would she let on that she'd imagined him as a merman.

"Ready to swim?" His eyes were almost the color of the water. Being wet also made his tanned skin seem darker. He would taste of salt, she suddenly thought, and had a fleeting image of licking that broad chest.

She dived under the breaking wave.

During the following hour Jake stayed with her, teaching her to read the waves. They arrived in sets, the earlier ones generally being softer than the later ones.

"You need to line up facing the shore," Jake explained. "Then when the wave comes, you swim like mad. It'll pick you up and carry you in."

It sounded easy, too easy.

"But how do I know which one to catch?" she asked.

"You'll learn to recognize them."

Sass didn't like having her back to the wave. "I can't see then if something's wrong."

"What could go wrong?"

"A shark. A lunatic surfer who hasn't seen me."

"You're going to have to learn to trust your instincts."

That made her smile. "I trust my instincts and

they are saying 'Sass Walker, you belong on land, girl!'"

Jake laughed. "You're a strong swimmer."

"I don't trust all this whitewash stuff."

"What's the worst that'll happen?"

"I'll be knocked down."

Which is exactly what happened the very next wave. She was swept off her feet and barreled up to shore in a terrifying tangle of salt, sand and limbs. It really was like being churned in a washing machine. She couldn't tell up from down, couldn't swim, couldn't breathe. Could only surrender to the waves and hope like hell they'd take her to shore. They did. She landed with a whack and was dragged and ground painfully over the sandy bottom. She came up spluttering, saltwater burning her throat so badly she could hardly talk. It stung to open her eyes. Then she felt a strong hand under her elbow, heard the twang of a Kiwi accent.

"That wasn't so bad, was it? You've just survived the worst that could happen, Ms. Walker."

"No." She coughed because of all the salt in her mouth. "I've just thought of something worse—*not* surfacing."

He helped her back on her feet. "I promise you, as long as I'm around, or one of the boys, we'll make sure you surface every time."

She was annoyed to find herself feeling grateful

to this patronizing male—not that he was patronizing as such. Protective maybe. And confident. Very, very sure of himself.

"Let's do it again," she said, determining then and there never to need rescuing. "Come on."

This time she was the one who waded in quicker, duck diving out to where the waves broke.

JAKE WATCHED HER forging ahead and had to hand it to her—she had guts. He'd seen her reservation, which had turned to alarm when she was wading out. And that had been quite a battering she'd taken, but still she was hell-bent on proving she could do it. Without his help.

She had an athletic build. Seeing her on that damned treadmill today had reminded him of how long her legs were, and now, watching her dive through the waves, he saw she had the grace of a woman used to her body obeying her. Aerobic classes, he guessed, and many laps at some indoor pool. She also had the mind and determination of an athlete. She might have found his interruption disconcerting this morning, but she hadn't stopped training. This had amused him but impressed him, too.

His thoughts strayed back to the previous evening. She'd been great with that social worker and the boys. When Sass forgot to be that uptown, uptight lawyer, she was warm and relaxed as a summer's night. And those twilight eyes of hers…

This morning he'd woken with a jolt and lain in bed for a while, analyzing the emotion that had pulled him out of sleep. It was, he'd realized, anticipation. Or apprehension. It was hard to tell, but clearly he needed to become better acquainted with the New Yorker. Because, he explained to himself, he was damned if he was going to be played the way the social worker had been. *Know thy enemy.* But then the way she'd laughed with the boys… Hell, he didn't know what he thought anymore. It hadn't been true that the boys had suggested inviting Sass; it had been his idea. His brief, he reminded himself, was to get her to fall in love with the land, see it through their eyes. But as he'd walked over to the sleep-out, his stomach had tightened in a way it hadn't since he'd been a teenager crazy with first love.

"This wave?" she called out, mercifully interrupting his train of thought.

"Yeah, swim!" he shouted. But though she went flat out, the wave passed beneath her.

"What went wrong?" she asked, disappointed, when he swam out to her.

"You missed it, that's all. It happens."

She missed the next two, got bowled over

again on the third—one he caught. She surfaced, spluttering.

"Man, I'm useless," she said, full of self-loathing. "This is way harder than it looks. And yet you caught it."

"I've lived in the water, remember."

"So how long does this game take to learn?"

"You'll get it soon enough."

"Yeah, yeah. I've heard that sort of talk before—from motivational bullshit artists!"

"Ouch. It was meant as encouragement."

"Well, I want to get out now."

"One last wave."

"No." She began wading back to shore.

"I'll show you another chapter."

She paused but didn't turn around. God, she really did have some body.

"Another chapter, and I'll introduce you to the best coffee shop in Whangarimu. They make great chocolate brownies."

At this she laughed and turned, her eyes as blue as the Pacific. "Cheap shot, but you'd make one tough prosecutor. Straight for the jugular. Okay, you've got yourself a deal."

Together they swam out again. Did she notice how well matched their strokes were? he wondered. The thought was strangely alluring. Definitely, this celibacy thing was getting out of control. And he'd been doing so well, too, until she'd stepped off the plane.

"Now what?" She treaded water and looked at him.

"Now we wait. See? The next set is coming through. We'll let the first couple of waves go under us."

"Okay." She flipped onto her back and floated spread-eagled on the water, eyes closed. "This feels amazing."

His jaw tightened, but he kept his voice light. "I think this is the first time I've seen you really relax."

She smiled, eyes still closed. "Don't be deceived. This is the face of a woman snatching her last minute of peace before being knocked against that damned beach again."

Jake laughed and watched as the wave lifted her on the swell, then lowered her. He had to look away, search for the second wave, to keep any semblance of logic in his head.

"Here it comes."

She righted herself and lined up as he'd shown her.

"We'll do this together," he said.

From the look in her eyes he could see she was apprehensive, but from the set of her mouth, he knew she wasn't about to beg off, either.

"Ready? Now!"

They both took off, he with his long reach, she with a furious, desperate stroke. The swell caught and lifted them. It was going to be a big wave. They were still side by side. "Keep kicking, then arrow!"

He'd yelled, but didn't know if she'd heard him as the wave peaked, and suddenly they were both sliding down the glassy face. A glance showed him that she was arrowed as he'd shown her, one arm stretched out, carving a path down the sleek water. Then they were scraping along the shoreline in the white salt froth of the spent wave.

Sass lay there for a second, the water dragging back down her body. Then she rolled over, her face alight with joy.

"That was simply incredible!"

And at that moment, as he fought the impulse to lean down and kiss those lips, he knew he was the one who was suddenly out of his depth, not Sass. And with shoals all around him.

CHAPTER EIGHT

AFTER BREAKFAST, Sass took off in her little sports car. When Jake had asked her what she had planned, she said, rather vaguely he thought for a hotshot lawyer, that there were things she wanted to check out in the library. Soon after, he drove Brad and Paul into town, before going on to work a few hours at the remote farm. Mac needed a new fence, and there was something about the jarring noise and vibration of the posthole borer that suited Jake's mood. If only he could bore out all thoughts and images of Miss Pain-in-the. He'd walked out of the kitchen when she'd been teaching the boys to make pancakes, unable to bear the sight of her winning them over with a judicious mix of toughness and kidding. They'd been putty in her hands. Jake was damned if he was going to fall so easily for Texan wiles.

Lost in his work, he hardly noticed the passing of time, and it was only when he happened to glance down at his watch that he realized how close he was cutting things. He was going to be late for parent interviews if he wasn't careful. Angry with himself and, quite unfairly, with Sass for occupying his thoughts, he packed up fast and began speeding back to town.

Exactly halfway between the farm and town, the van's rackety engine coughed and died. Swearing, Jake hopped out of the vehicle. But after fiddling with the motor and getting covered in oil, he discovered the power coil had gone and that he'd have to call for a tow. Of all the worst possible times. He texted Brad, knowing Paul's phone had died a week earlier. No response. He tried ringing. Mark answered.

"What the hell? Where's Brad?"

He could practically hear Mark's shrug as he said, "He's still in town. He forgot his phone."

Great. Rob and Moana were away for the day, and for a minute Jake agonized. He simply couldn't afford to look bad in front of Janet again. There was only one thing to do.

She answered on the first ring.

"Sass? Are you still in town? Good. Look, I'm in a bind. The van's broken down in the middle of nowhere. I'll get hold of AA but I'm going to be late for the boys' interviews. Can you warn them? They haven't got their phones with them. Maybe some could be rescheduled for later."

"Sure, no problem. Leave it to me."

She rang off, just like that. Jake glared at his phone, then gave the wheel a hefty kick. Swearing under his breath, he began punching the number of the AA, which he'd come to learn by heart.

JAKE ARRIVED very late and filthy. As he entered the school hall the din hit him like a physical blow. Teachers were lined in rows the length of the hall, each facing two chairs filled with nodding, questioning parents. Parents also lined the walls, while boys milled about, laughing and pushing each other. There must have been at least five hundred people in the crowded space. It was his worst nightmare. Even walking into school gave him the heebie-jeebies. Uniforms, rules, expectations. He loathed the lot.

Brad materialized at his elbow. "There you are. Told you the van needed an overhaul."

He was just trying to get a rise and Jake bit back a rejoinder, saying irritably instead, "So where's the appointment list? Did you reschedule? Where the hell is Paul?"

"Relax, man. Sass has got both lists and is managing fine."

"*What?*" Jake spun around, searching the hall, and yes, there she was. How could he have missed her before? There was one ray of sunlight slanting through the high windows and of course Sass was sitting right in its path, her angel-gold hair twisted into a neat bun. She was wearing a straight yellow skirt that stopped just above the knee and a sleeveless, white cotton blouse. If she'd been going for casual, she'd missed it by a mile. He paused, trying to align this vision with her tales of a trailer park upbringing.

"Pretty hot, ay?" said Brad.

Jake shot him a dark look, but knew he couldn't be upset at Brad for voicing thoughts that would be going through the minds of every man in the room. "Coming?" he asked succinctly.

"No way. The teachers'll enjoy bitching about me better behind my back."

Jake struggled up the aisle, squeezing past the chairs. Sass was deep in conversation and didn't notice him, so he stood back, waiting for the interview to finish. From the label on the teacher's desk, he learned she was talking to Mrs. Frazer, English. They were so engrossed that they jumped when the timer on the desk went off, making them both laugh.

"It was lovely meeting you, Sass," said Mrs. Frazer, and Jake just knew Paul had shifted onto her list of favorites.

As Sass rose, she caught sight of him. Her eyes widened as she took in his oil-stained T-shirt, his blackened hands and dusty boots. But all she said was, "I'm glad you've made it. Now, you're here on Paul's list and here on Brad's list." She pushed two papers into his hands, both horribly crumpled from several days' incarceration in boys' pockets.

Jake tried to seem gracious. "Thanks for picking this up, but you really didn't have to."

"Don't worry about it. I've only done the one interview. I explained the situation and was going to reschedule, but Mrs. Frazer said she didn't have anything confidential, so we chatted away. I've got some real interesting things to tell you, but you'd better get a move on now or you'll miss your appointment with Mr. Braithwaite. He's over there. I checked out the teachers' seatings right at the beginning."

"Of course you did." Then, seeing her expression, Jake said, "Oh, come on. I can see you're dying to meet him."

"Can I?" Her eyes were still that incredible blue, even in this dim hall. "I confess I'm curious. Brad hates him and I'd love to see if it's mutual."

"I'm sure it is," said Jake as he fought his way across to the next aisle.

"But who is the more justified?"

Mr. Braithwaite took one look at Jake's disheveled appearance and turned his attention to Sass. Jake was annoyed at being summarily dismissed, but at the same time he wanted to see Sass deal with conflict. Information that could prove very useful. By the end of the first minute, he was disappointed. She allowed Braithwaite not only to patronize her but also to move swiftly into bully-teacher mode, listing an impressive array of Brad's misdemeanors. In the second minute she examined the column of Brad's poor results. In the third minute she extracted a list of coming assignments and tests, and promised it would be displayed prominently in the house. She was *rolling over.* Despite his disgust in seeing how easily she caved, Jake felt rising optimism for their own chances in negotiating with her.

In the final two minutes Sass engaged Braithwaite in a brief but efficient conversation on the joys of physics and teaching methodologies in New Zealand. It was hard to see exactly how she did it, but by the fifty-ninth second of the final minute the teacher had, seemingly by himself, outlined a range of strategies that could be used to keep highly spirited, intelligent young men engaged in their studies. Sass pushed back her chair and rose, smiling.

"Those sound like mighty fine ways to teach, Mr. Braithwaite. I'm looking forward to Bradley coming home and telling us all about them. With classes like that, I'm sure he'll give you no trouble at all."

Having firmly put all the responsibility back onto Braithwaite, she wished him a "nice day now" and departed.

"Well," said Jake as they pushed their way to the next appointment. "He certainly didn't see *that* coming. Neither did I, for that matter."

Sass smiled. "My mom's a teacher. I grew up listening to teacherspeak. Come on, time for the next appointment."

"You're enjoying this!"

"Sure, it's fun finding out how the boys are doing."

Jake could think of a lot better ways of having fun, but Sass was in her element. She had Head Girl written all over her, though her concern for the boys seemed sincere. He'd also realized that it wasn't calculated charm that people succumbed to when talking to her, it was her real interest in listening to what they had to say. Which made her nicer than he liked to admit, but also a far more dangerous opponent.

The rest of the interviews sped by, blurring into earnest teacher faces, columns of results and a litany of complaints about Brad. Paul had slipped under the radar for the most part, as quiet, well-behaved boys so often did.

The boys were nowhere to be seen when Sass and Jake went outside so, sitting side by side on the school wall, they discussed everything they'd just heard.

"Paul's doing okay in all his subjects, but he could probably raise his game," Sass said. "Because he's a well-behaved kid, he can get away with the minimum of work."

"He's passing."

Sass pursed her lips. "Not good enough. He's bright. Encourage him and you'll see his grades rise."

Jake braced his hands on either side of his body, shifting his butt on the rough wall. "I'll try, but I have the feeling you're the one he'd respond to. He's getting under your skin, isn't he?"

She laughed. "Yeah, there's something about him that makes me want to wrap him up and take him home."

"I'll have Customs search you before you leave." Jake became serious. "Brad's clearly not settling down."

"He's also bright, but needs a boot up the ass."

"I was wondering if school's the wrong place for him."

"No way!" Sass glared at Jake. "If he leaves now, what're his prospects? If he sticks at school for one more year, then he'll have a lot more options."

"I'm not sure he'll be able to stand a year of it."

"You've got to make him stand it."

"You sound like my father when *I* wanted to leave school."

"What will he do instead? Become a surfing champ like you did?"

Jake sighed, exasperated. "God knows he could if he wanted. But he lacks commitment. I don't get it. There are kids around the country who'd give their eye teeth for a quarter of his talent, yet he refuses to get serious. Such a bloody waste."

"Talk to him."

Jake gave a short laugh. "You think I haven't tried?"

"Yeah, I know that one, all right." Her voice was surprisingly bitter and she immediately bit her lip.

"Your brothers?"

Her nod was barely discernable. She didn't meet his eyes.

"I've been wondering how you ended up a lawyer while they went off the straight and narrow."

"Long story," she said in a tone that did not invite further questions.

Jake had not, however, become a champion by giving up. "Also, if there was no money, how did you pay for university? I thought it cost a bomb to go in the States."

"A scholarship."

"And?" he persisted in a deceptively friendly tone.

"I did some modeling."

"Really?" He kept his voice as casual as hers. "What sort of modeling?"

She shrugged. "This and that."

"What, like fashion shows?"

"No, nothing in that league." She looked down the street. "What time is it, anyway? Those boys are late."

He couldn't believe she'd try such a lame tactic. "Swimsuits?"

She threw him an oh-come-on look, but her cheeks turned faintly pink.

"Life drawing classes?" She shook her head, but there was definitely a wariness in her eyes and he feigned shock. "Oh my God, not—not *Playboy?*"

"No!" she said, outraged. "I did underwear for Wal-Mart catalogs, okay?" Then she closed her eyes. Jake sat back and grinned. *Yes.*

Sass shook her head. "Jeez, I've never told *anyone* before."

He laughed. "What's the big deal? It's nothing to be ashamed of. Quite the contrary."

She snorted. "Yeah, right. And what would people say if they knew?" She leaned toward him, her face deadly serious, and waved an admonishing finger under his nose. "If you breathe one word of this..."

She was only mock threatening him, but Jake

was thrown by the entreaty he heard beneath it. Suddenly he saw things from her point of view. If Whangarimu learned of this, her credibility might take a hit. How could a woman look tough, defiant, proud and vulnerable all at the same time? His sense of triumph evaporated and now it was his turn to feel outraged. Did she honestly think he was the same sort of lowlife as that bastard Branston?

"Of course I won't tell," he said, aggrieved.

She stared at him, then nodded. "Thanks."

Still ruffled, he was not about to let her off that easily. "Yeah, well, my silence has to be bought."

She leaned back and arched an eyebrow. "I demand a peek at a couple of said catalogs."

"Over my dead body." But she was smiling now, her real smile. He smiled back and at that moment he could have sworn something between them shifted. But before Jake could put a name to it, Sass pointed. "Hey, look, here come the boys."

Brad and Paul were loping toward them. Just as well, he told himself as he stood and tried to dismiss the peculiar mix of emotions coursing through his system. Whatever the hell had just happened, she was still the enemy.

CHAPTER NINE

THERE WERE A FEW HOURS until the meeting that night and as Sass cooked dinner, she reviewed the afternoon. She'd enjoyed becoming involved with the boys, and the chat with Jake had been great, right up until she'd opened her big mouth. But instead of seizing this advantage, he'd seemed offended she might think he'd use it against her.

All the way home they'd joked with the boys, with each other, using humor to bury whatever had passed between them. Jake was clearly as keen as she was to put it behind them.

Sass served dinner early and enjoyed the way the boys devoured it. It felt good, surprisingly good, to feel part of their camaraderie. She was reminded of the times when her mom got her act straight and they'd set up the trestle table and sit down outside, under the stars of the wide Texan skies, and behave just like a regular family. There hadn't been nearly enough occasions like that, though.

At the end of the meal the boys leaped up, and

while the twins cleared the table, Paul and Brad went into the kitchen, squabbling over who would stack the dishwasher and who would wash the pans. Jake watched them go.

"Okay, what sorcery are you using this time?"

"Magic isn't required. It's all very well being too cool for rules, Jake, but what you are witnessing are routines in action. While we were making pancakes this morning, we discussed tasks and lines of responsibility. Each boy had to sign up for something or cook his own meals. You should have done that the minute they walked into the house. No wonder they sit around waiting for you to baby them."

Jake leaned back, folding his arms over his chest. It made his T-shirt strain across the shoulders. Even in small gestures he exuded a sense of harnessed power. "I've *never* seen myself as a nursemaid!"

"You don't know how to see yourself, that's your problem. You guys entered into this situation without sorting out the fine print. No wonder things were getting out of control." But before he could start mustering arguments, she fixed him with her best courtroom stare and tapped the table. "The time has come, Jake Finlayson, for you to honor our deal."

He lost his cocky stance and shifted his eyes as if trying to find the way out of a hole. "What deal?"

"Cut the crap. I want the book. I need to find out more about these birds you're hell-bent on saving."

She watched the tide of red rising up his neck. He put on a convincing macho act, but this guy definitely had his weaknesses. Problem was, instead of feeling scornful, Sass was dismayed to find it kind of cute. Then his eyes narrowed. He was never down for long.

"Yeah, well, deal's a deal, I guess." He uncoiled from his chair. "Besides, it probably wouldn't hurt you to learn something about the birds you are so keen to destroy."

"Oh, good grief." She rolled her eyes, but he'd already left the room. Jake talked as if she were some kind of ax murderer, but Kurt had already told her they were only talking seven birds here. How much of a deal could this guy make of that?

Jake emerged a few minutes later with a bird's nest of mismatched papers sticking out at different angles.

"Jeez, what happened? Cyclone hit your room?"

He shrugged. "I haven't figured out a filing system yet."

Sass shuffled through the pile. "But you haven't numbered the pages. Some haven't even been typed up. How do you know what's what?"

"Look, I didn't want to show you the bloody thing in the first place."

She'd hit a nerve. "Sorry, you're right. You sort it out. I'll just shut up and read."

He was only slightly mollified. "Well, these are the first three chapters I showed to the publisher, and they accepted the book on them."

These pages were formatted, but dog-eared and creased. She forbore making comments, however, as she banged the pile into shape on the table before she began reading. The first paragraph shocked a small, involuntary gasp out of her. Jake glanced up from the papers he was sorting.

Sass stared at the page in front of her. "Are these figures right? It says here, 'There are only between thirty-five and forty fairy terns left in the world.'"

"Yeah, that's right, give or take a few each season. What? Didn't Branston spell that out to you?"

"So when we talk about seven birds…" said Sass slowly.

"That's right. We're talking about your company destroying almost twenty percent, just like that."

"Oh, come on, it's not quite like that." He cocked his head skeptically. Needled, she added, "Just let me read, okay?"

For the next ten minutes, Sass read in silence. The facts were bleak, far bleaker than that slimeball had presented to The Boys. This changed things, but she couldn't let Jake know that until she'd had time to properly think it through. She decided, as she read, to focus their discussions on him and his writing. That would keep the guy off-kilter.

At the end, she put the papers down and leaned back in her chair. "So far, so good. I can see why the publisher accepted the book. It's factual and informative."

"You didn't like it."

She bit her lip. "I'm not your target audience, okay? Nothing personal, but a bird book would be just about my last choice, normally. However, I can see you know your stuff, and that's what counts. So what's your problem with finishing?"

Jake couldn't meet her eyes. "Things changed."

"Changed how?"

"Stylistically," he muttered, shoving the next wad of papers at her. "You'll see. I haven't had a chance to type these pages up yet."

It took her a few minutes to get used to the sprawling handwriting—a handwriting analyst would have a field day with the strong upward and downward strokes, the looping fluidity—but none of that counted by the end of the second page. In this chapter, Jake was recording the hatching of two chicks. It began with the same dry factual tone as the previous chapter, but as he sought words to describe their fragility, the miracle of their hatching his writing began to shift. Words began to pour forth, filling page after page, as he described their development on an almost daily basis.

Then another pair of terns had two chicks hatch. Eventually, eight baby terns in all, but not just birds, characters in their own right. Jake had an excellent eye for detail, yet it was more than that. Underneath the narrative ran a current of affectionate humor that lifted the pages out of ornithological manuals and into popular nonfiction. It was lucky for her company, she thought, that it wouldn't be published before the resort went in.

Then came the part where one of the chicks disappeared, taken by a stoat. Jake trapped and killed the predator the following day, but his pain at being too late to save the baby came through clearly. The words blurred in front of her and without thinking Sass said, "Jake, this is brilliant!"

While she'd been reading, he'd been sorting papers, though she'd been aware of him glancing in her direction from time to time.

"You like it?" As always, he sounded confident, but she saw the insecurity in his eyes.

"Yeah, I do. I really like it." She saw hope flare in those green depths and felt compelled to add, "It's as if you gave up trying to be a professor and just wrote. I love the way you describe the birds as individual characters. It's funny and touching."

Jake set the pages in his hand on the table. "But it's not what the publishers think they're getting. It's completely different from the early chapters."

Sass leaned forward to make her point. "It's way, way better."

"You don't find it…" he searched for words "…soft?"

She laughed. "So that's it. Doesn't fit your macho image, right?"

"Shaddup," he growled, but his lips twitched. "So you honestly think it's okay? I didn't know what to think when the book started developing this life of its own. I tried to get back to my earlier style, but then everything became stilted—awful, really."

"It's infinitely better than the beginning." Seeing his expression, she amended that quickly. "The first chapters were good, of course, but they're just like all the other bird books I've never really wanted to read. This—" she tapped the pile in front of her "—is both funny and touching. Your descriptions of the bay are pretty damned poetic, too."

He groaned. "For God's sake, don't tell the boys. They'll never let me live *that* down."

"So," said Sass, getting down to business, "where are you at? You've got a lot here. Much more to write?"

He shook his head. "No, it's just a short book. It needs more on the fledglings leaving the nest, and then a bit at the end, spelling out what needs to be done to save the terns. I guess I'll also need to rewrite the first few chapters so they fit better stylistically. The biggest time waster will be typing up the handwritten sections and getting all my files in order. I've printed as I've gone, but it's a shambles on the computer. Then, of course, I can't write the final chapter until…"

Of course. He couldn't write the final chapter until he knew the fate of the spit. In that moment, they slipped from warmth back to confrontation. This time it stung more than it had before. It wasn't as though she personally wanted to murder his birds. But clearly, he'd hold her responsible for whatever happened to them.

"Jake, look, we'll make provisions—fence the spit off, put up trespass signs."

He shook his head. "You don't get it. Their world is as fragile as their bodies. The slightest disturbances leave them vulnerable. For example, I saw in your plan that windsurfing and Jet Skis would be offered in the harbor."

She shrugged. "Sure. What's that got to do with their nesting?"

Jake laced his fingers together, leaning forward on his forearms. "The terns aren't territorial about the land, but they are about the waters they fish in."

"Yeah, I remember that part. You wrote that it's almost possible to draw circles in the water, marking the fishing grounds of the pairs of parents."

Jake nodded. "That's right. They also won't fish while there is any activity, especially human activity, near their territory. Think how that will affect them in the summer, when your resort is at its busiest and when, incidentally, the chicks hatch."

"We can steer people away from those areas."

Jake leaned back and shook his head. "And who's going to monitor it, day in, day out? C'mon, Sass, I may have been naive about how much work four boys generate, but even I can see that a horde of holiday-makers, even those with the best of intentions, aren't going to pay much mind to—how did you put it?—a handful of birds."

Sass frowned. "There'll be a way around this."

"What?"

The word was bald, hard, uncompromising.

"I don't know." She was rattled to hear herself sounding defensive. "We could relocate the birds."

"Yeah, we could try. It doesn't have a high success rate, though. Remember, we are talking twenty percent of all the fairy terns in the world. Can't afford to dick around too much with them."

"Even so," she said, "there's got to be a solution. There always is."

"There is. Don't build the bloody resort."

The silence between them was cold. Jake leaned back, watching her, his jaw set, arms once more folded across his chest.

"Look, Jake, I'm not here to destroy some bird families just for the hell of it."

"No," he conceded. "Not for the hell of it, perhaps, but certainly for a multimillion dollar resort."

She knew it was pointless to go on at this moment. *Wrap up, leave it on a positive note.* She smiled disarmingly.

"Point taken. Thanks for letting me read your book. I learned a lot. It's good, it's really good." He slanted a skeptical look at her and she laughed. "How about I offer to help organize this book while I'm here."

His eyes narrowed. "Why would you do that?"

"A gesture of goodwill, as I said. To put my money where my mouth is. I think it's a great book, but you've got no system to how you work. No patterns of organization. They're my forte. We have an hour now before I need to get ready for the meeting. How about it?"

He was caught off guard. The start to winning people over was by acting contrary to their expectations. Get them doubting themselves. Sass didn't feel bad. It was a promising book; she could help him. And if it helped her case, too, well, win-win.

"C'mon, Jake, surely you'll find satisfaction in using me for your own ends."

Unexpectedly, that did it. He laughed and uncrossed his arms. "You're right. May as well use you while I can."

"Great. I'll go get my laptop."

Sass left the room and for a second Jake stared after her. She'd seemed both so sincere and so wry in making her offer that he'd barely stopped himself from leaning forward to touch her hair. God, she was a dangerous opponent. He knew thoughts were spinning through that analytical brain of hers, but nothing registered on her smooth face. Part of him admired her control, part of him itched to smash it all to hell. But she was offering a truce. For the moment, he had to go with that. Be nice. Woo her into seeing Aroha Bay as they saw it. Outright opposition wouldn't help.

Jake rose and went through to the kitchen, where the boys were finishing up. The place was unrecognizable. When he plugged in Sass's coffee machine, however, it was the boys' turn to be surprised.

"Whattaya doing?" Brad asked.

"Making coffee, Einstein."

"But you hate coffee and you hate that machine," Mark pointed out.

Jake shrugged as he got out the instruction book. "Sometimes, boys, you have to move out of your comfort zone."

"Yeah, right." Brad had a knowing grin. Jake picked up a wet tea towel and flicked it hard at the wise guy.

"Go on, get out of here. If I blow the thing up, I don't want blood on my hands."

As the boys trooped out, laughing, he overheard Brad say, "Bet they hook up in the next three days."

SASS WAS SETTING UP her computer when he came back into the dining room. She'd put on a pair of glasses that immediately provoked memories of corny movies where the plain secretary turned into a sex goddess. He handed her a steaming mug.

"Is that— My God, it is! I thought you didn't make coffee?"

"I *can* follow instructions, though."

"Only when it suits you." She took a sip and her eyes widened. "Wow, this is okay for a first-timer!"

"Yeah, well, it's not rocket science," he said, pulling out a chair and settling into it, his own mug of tea at his elbow. “And I thought the least I could do was give you a caffeine fix to keep you going.”

He knew she’d love a nicotine fix, too. Tough. She’d just have to do that furtively before she went to bed.

Her head was already bent over the screen. He hated to admit it, but if felt companionable working side by side like this. For the second time that day he found himself wondering what would have happened if they’d met under different circumstances. But they hadn’t.

Jake returned to work, aware of a twinge of something almost like regret.

CHAPTER TEN

LINGERING TWILIGHT HAD just deepened into night when Jake and Sass arrived to pick up Rob and Moana for the meeting.

"I hear there was trouble with the VW today," Rob said as he climbed into the Jeep.

Jake groaned. "Oh, God! Is it all around town?"

"Yup, the gossips loved the idea of our surf champ stranded high and dry," Moana said, buckling in.

"I also hear that Sass went down a treat at the school."

"How small is this town?" she exclaimed.

Moana laughed. "Small enough for everyone not only to know you sneezed, but the hour and minute you did so."

"Oh, man, I'd better watch out. But the gossip is wrong. I didn't do anything special at the interviews."

Jake shifted gears as he pulled away from the curb. "Actually, much as I hate to admit it, you did a great job there. The teachers were eating out of your hand." Looking at his brother in the rearview mirror, he added, "She's good. We'll have to watch our backs."

Before Sass could protest, Rob said in his easy way, "From many others tonight, too, I suspect."

Moana leaned forward, her arms along the top of Jake's seat, her head turned to Sass, eyes full of mischief. "Have you brought along an asbestos suit?"

"Why? Are the townsfolk going to turn ugly toward me?"

"Nah, it's not that. It's Jake and his dad. Things can get pretty hot when they're in the same room."

"It's his fault," Jake stated. "He's the most intractable individual in the world."

Rob laughed. "Says Mr. Reasonable Compromise."

Jake eyeballed his brother in the mirror. "I'm not a pushover like some I know."

Moana patted Jake's shoulder. "There, there," she said. Then she turned back to Sass. "Jake gets damned prickly whenever he's with his father. It's because they're so similar. Jake's just a chip off the old, bloody-minded block."

"Oh, God, take me out and shoot me now if that's the truth." But Jake was laughing and the rest of the trip flew by. Sass realized that she felt completely at home with these people she'd met only a few days earlier. It seemed no time at all before they were pulling into the car park, which was already packed with vehicles.

"Perfect timing," Rob said. "There are the parents."

A distinguished-looking couple had just climbed out of an obviously new Audi TT and were making their way across to the Jeep.

"Jake! Rob!" The woman pounced on her sons and then hugged Moana.

"I'm Matt Finlayson," the man said, giving Sass a no-nonsense handshake. "You must be the hotshot lawyer come to talk sense into my boys. Should be an interesting meeting tonight. I've been telling Jake he's wasting his time, but as always, he knows best. I'd expected Rob to be reasonable, though."

He was as tall as his sons, with powerful shoulders. But his hair was silver and his face had a hardness that Sass had not seen in Jake's, even at his most belligerent. Everything about him spoke of wealth and confidence. Sass felt suddenly awkward, realizing that she'd completely bought into Jake's hokey surfer image.

She hid it well, though, as she gave her standard reply, "I'm just here to listen, Mr. Finlayson. My company wants everyone to have the chance to express their view."

"Oh, come, you don't really expect us to believe that? It's a charade to placate the irate locals, after which your company'll steam ahead—isn't that right?" It was uncomfortably close to the truth. "Look, I don't blame you," he said. "I'm in business myself. Shopping malls. I keep telling Jake he might as well stand in the path of an oncoming tanker as try to stop your company."

Sass saw Jake stiffen. His father saw it, too.

"There you go, pokering up. Don't get tetchy because I say it like it is." He turned back to Sass, shaking his head. "Jake's always so quick to take offense," he said, as though bewildered by this unaccountable behavior.

Inwardly, Sass sighed. Her job would be a whole lot easier if Père Finlayson wasn't taking her side. She was saved from replying, however, as Jake's mother cut in.

"So lovely to meet you, Sass. I'm Margot."

Jake had inherited his bright eyes from her and, when he wasn't being defensive, her particularly warm smile. She embraced Sass, which was surprising. But also nice. Then she stepped back. "Shall we go in?"

Margot took Matt's arm. Moana slipped her hand into Rob's. For a fleeting second, Sass envied them. But as she started in alone, she felt

Jake's hand on her back, warm through her silk blouse.

"This way." His slight pressure guided her up the steps and into the hall. It was impossible to tell from his expression if this was a proprietary gesture to alarm the ABORD supporters or whether he was being kind.

The hall was a reasonable size, but very plain, with whitewashed walls, high windows and a stage at the far end. Shabby velvet curtains had faded from royal purple to dusty grape. Seating ranged from old-fashioned benches at the front to as many hard, wooden chairs as could be squeezed in. The air vibrated with excitement as hundreds of people greeted one another. It might be a divided community, but it was nevertheless a close one.

"Now, the main speakers will be up on the stage. We've put a seat there for you, too," Jake said, stooping to speak into Sass's ear to make himself heard. His breath was hot, setting her nerves tingling.

"I'd rather be in the audience," she replied.

"But you're the guest of honor."

"Thanks, but this evening isn't about me, it's about Whangarimu."

He seemed about to disagree, but she put a palm on his arm. "Please."

He looked down at her hand, then into her eyes.

"If you're sure. But we will introduce you. Everyone will be dying to see what you're like."

"Of course." She removed her hand now that she had her way. Strong men, like horses, sometimes needed leading by touch.

Sass had her reasons for being in the audience. She would have a better view of the speakers, for a start, but more importantly, it would align her with the townspeople, make her one of them. She didn't want to distance herself or set herself higher, even in the most innocuous way. It also set her apart from the antiresort constituents reinforcing her policy of being here to listen impartially.

"Come and meet the mayor, then," Jake said, his hand again going to the small of her back, while he added over his shoulder to Moana, "Save a place in the front row for Sass."

Guiding her past the throng's curious glances, Jake led her up on stage, where he introduced her to the mayor, an untidy man with a paunch.

"Delighted to meet you, Sass," he said, his gaze dropping to her breasts. "I'm sorry I've been out of town or I'd have made your acquaintance sooner."

"Golf, was it, Tom?" Jake asked innocently.

The mayor shot him a look. "No, no. Mayoral business," he said, his hand making a vague circle in the air. "I hope we'll have lots of time to get better acquainted."

"Yes, but not now," Jake stated. "We should get this meeting started."

"True, true." The mayor smiled at Sass. "Duty never done and all that." Giving her arm a squeeze, he added sotto voce, "We'll talk later," before bustling off to the podium.

Jake's glare bore a hole in the mayor's back before he went to join Rob and the other speakers onstage. Tom stepped forward, raising both hands to silence the audience. It took a few minutes before he was noticed, but gradually the noise fell away. He then welcomed everyone, outlined the reason for the meeting and the order in which the speakers would talk.

"But before we begin, it is my great pleasure," he said, "to introduce you to Sass Walker, who has come all the way from New York. We are lucky indeed to have such a beautiful young woman to listen to us."

Sass saw Jake roll his eyes, but she was used to men initially dismissing her because of her looks. Jake hadn't, she suddenly realized as she stepped up to the podium. He'd hated her, but he hadn't dismissed her.

For a moment, Sass stood looking out over the blur of faces. She'd already decided on her strategy of keeping a sympathetic but low profile. Kurt always made the mistake of trying to dominate. In contrast, Sass kept her speech simple, expressing her delight to be there, thanking the town for their welcome and reiterating her role as listener.

"I really do want to hear from you." And she meant it. Persuader or manipulator, in the end she knew her greatest skill lay in finding a compromise that appeased everyone. Tonight she was going to find out exactly how hard that might be in this case.

The applause as she took her seat was restrained, but at least she hadn't been booed. This, she felt, was a reasonable start, and she settled next to Moana, who whispered, "Wow, Sass. Another few minutes of that Southern charm and you'd have had the whole audience eating out of your hand. Even I forgot for a minute that we're sworn enemies."

"Moana!" Margot whispered, but Sass just smiled.

THE FIRST SPEAKER WAS Manu Rihari, from the ABORD Committee. He was a tall, well-built Māori with a soft voice and shrewd intelligence. Sass leaned forward, feeling lighter. This man was her ally.

"My friends," he began, "it saddens my heart that we are, for the first time I can remember, a deeply divided community. Whangarimu and her environs are dear to all of us, but we must be realistic. Our town is dying."

Manu went on to enumerate the businesses that had closed down over the past ten years, quoted the statistics of ever rising unemployment.

"This resort is a lifeline to our town, to our people. We must seize it."

He took his seat amid wild applause from some and muted heckling from others.

The next speaker was an engineer who spoke confidently about the feasibility of installing sewage and water systems in Aroha Bay. He was followed by an environmentalist who discussed the disruption this process would have on the ancient tree root systems and the soft-earth cliffs. Both speakers had the same mixed response that Manu had evoked, though it got louder each time.

A Māori woman, bent with age and dressed in an ankle-length, faded floral skirt shuffled forward. She had an indefinable quality that immediately caught Sass's attention, and the room fell silent as she talked about their ancestors who had built the pā and the great battles the site had seen. She went overtime, but the applause at the end was loud and unqualified.

A young man with a bright tie came forward next. This must be Andy, the entrepreneur Kurt had recommended as the only one with vision in the town.

"This is our chance to put Whangarimu on the map," he urged. "The resort it just the beginning."

He went on to expand on his dream of Whangarimu becoming *the* holiday destination of New Zealand, with a large fun fair and casino to follow.

Sass was torn between being appalled that Andy was an ally and feeling sorry for this babe in the big bad woods, ripe for fleecing by, well, types like Kurt.

Suddenly she had the unaccountable feeling that she was being watched. She glanced up to find Jake staring straight at her. He raised his eyebrows, inviting her to share in the joke. Then Moana shifted and the swing of her hair momentarily blocked Sass's view. When she looked again, Jake was gazing at Andy, face impassive.

The young man had gone on too long. Sass was aware of people stirring behind her. There was a lot of shuffling and the odd sound of chairs scraping the wooden floor. Another few minutes and the audience would turn ugly. Unwittingly, he was poisoning the meeting, polarizing divisions and thus making her job that much harder.

She saw Jake lean forward and whisper urgently to the mayor, who immediately rose.

"Thank you, Andy, but I'm afraid I'll have to stop you there or the meeting will go on all night. Now, it has just been suggested that some members of the audience might like to have a turn to speak after so much listening. We've only one speaker left and he's happy to wait."

It was an excellent move, allowing the crowd to vent. People bounced to their feet, one after another, to support the protection of the pa, to demand jobs, to proclaim the rights of free market, to insist that Whangarimu remain the same, that it change with the times, that it resist American domination and that it embrace the real world. For a faltering second, Sass wondered how on earth she would ever find a compromise. Then Matt Finlayson stood up and his presence seemed to fill the room.

"It is absurd," he said, his strong voice carrying the confidence of the highly successful, "to even be having this meeting. New Zealand is full of untouched, picturesque bays. What it needs is a positive way forward, a way to provide jobs, bring money into a depressed economy and stop the flight of our young to the cities. We wouldn't be discussing this now if it weren't for a few bleeding-heart environmentalists—" he shot a look directly at Jake "—who mistakenly believe they can save a handful of birds at the expense of progress. It's time to get real. Time, Whangarimu, to pull ourselves out of the fiscal doldrums and into prosperity and plenty."

The audience broke into an uproar. Cheers and

applause vied with angry cries, and when Sass turned around, she saw some raised fists. She breathed in sharply. This was exactly what she didn't want. Instead of feeling grateful to Matt for his support, she was angry. He'd whipped the already high feelings into a frenzy. How could they ever have a rational discussion now?

But beside her, Moana chuckled. "Jake's dander is up. You watch now."

Sass looked across at the brothers. Sure enough, Rob had remained calm, but Jake's jaw was set, his eyes blazing. He radiated such suppressed energy and fury that Sass half expected to see lightning crackle around his blond head.

"Thank you, Matt," said Tom, again stepping forward and trying to shout over the hubbub. "On that note, the man who needs no introduction—Jake Finlayson."

The noise crescendoed as whistling and stamping were added to the shouts of the audience. Jake rose and walked to the front of the stage. He nodded to Rob, who moved across to switch out the lights, and a screen was lowered. In the glow, Jake stood very still. He was an imposing figure despite the faded jeans, ragged around the hems. As a concession to formality, he'd worn a white shirt, which made his tan seem more golden than ever. His unruly mop of curls glinted. He stood with feet planted apart, hands tucked into back pockets, elbows taut—a gunslinger ready to take on the whole darn town. The noise died without him making a single gesture, a single sound. Then he turned and switched on the first slide. It was a drawing of a huge eagle.

"This was the New Zealand giant eagle, the biggest there has ever been on earth." Jake's voice revealed none of the fury she'd seen in his face just seconds earlier. "Its wingspan was up to three meters long. That's the distance from that window up there—" he gestured to one high on the wall, and everyone obediently looked up "—and reached all the way over to that beam." All eyes followed the large path as people took in the phenomenal dimensions. Jake smiled.

"The talons were huge." His hands measured the size in the air. "And would have been hanging low—just about…" he paused as though considering "…yeah, just about there—" his finger pointed "—right above my father's head."

He winked and everyone laughed, all ugliness dissolving instantly. Sass felt the breath leave her body in a long, slow exhalation. The tense lines under Jake's shirt also relaxed as he rocked back on his heels, a lecturer now sure of his audience's complete attention. "And that's only the beginning. I'm going to take you on a brief tour of all the birds New Zealand has lost over the centuries and, most tragically, over the past hundred years, thanks to mankind and his thoughtless or, worse, rapacious ways."

It was not a grim talk, though. Jake injected every slide with humor and interest, displaying a genius for highlighting details guaranteed to catch the imagination and make the birds come vividly alive. The list was dizzying: the moa, the laughing owl, the Stephens Island wren, the huia, the piopio, the Chatham Island bellbird, the South Island kōkako. Though people laughed at Jake's descriptions, Sass could hear the hitch in throats as his talk gathered momentum, moving on to the current gravely endangered species and finishing up, not surprisingly, with the fairy tern. The slide showed a pretty bird, white with a black head and bright orange legs and beak.

"Yes, we have many species of tern," Jake said. "Yes, the world will continue without these lovely birds, but…" he paused and the room was deathly quiet "…it will be that much emptier. As our lives are poorer without the birds we have already lost. My father was right. New Zealand abounds in unspoiled bays. Why then must we choose this one, one of the last sanctuaries for the fairy tern, for some resort, paid for with foreign dollars?"

Then, very deliberately, he turned to look at Sass. There was no warmth, no laughter in his expression now.

"It's time to make a stand for those creatures that cannot defend themselves. It's time for us to say no. No to greed, no to extinction. We must unite in our determination to preserve life, to preserve what is ours. Together we must go forward to stop these people who threaten Aroha Bay and the terns and drive them from our shores."

CHAPTER ELEVEN

THE JEEP WAS VERY QUIET after they dropped Rob and Moana off. The euphoria following his performance had faded and Jake felt drained.

He wasn't used to having a guilty conscience. He'd meant every word of what he'd said—of course he had. But now, with just the two of them, he couldn't help wondering what Sass was thinking. When he'd gazed directly at her in the hall, she'd looked right back at him, and for a second he'd felt as if he was in one of those movies where the background goes out of focus and the surrounding noises blur. Just Sass and himself, caught in a moment that stretched forever, yet was over in a flash.

Real life had swept in with tumultuous applause, and afterward he'd been inundated with well-wishers shaking his hand, slapping his back. Sass had accidentally been jostled by some of his supporters, and though apologies had been made immediately, it was as if he'd made her invisible.

Some of her hair had come out of the bun and Jake found himself thinking that it made Sass, usually so immaculate, seem vulnerable.

He stole a glance at his passenger. Her profile was rimmed in gold from the passing streetlights, her expression pensive as she stared into the darkness.

"Did you find the meeting helpful?" he asked.

"Very."

He cleared his throat. "What I said—it wasn't personal."

"Wasn't it?" she asked.

He didn't know how to answer truthfully.

They turned off the city streets onto the dark road leading home. Was she mad at him? What if she began to cry? He couldn't stop himself from asking the most clichéd question in all of history.

"So what are you thinking?"

She smiled. She had a really nice smile. "I was wondering whether Matt made his speech to damage your case or to help you."

His shoulders relaxed. She wasn't going to make a scene. Instead, like a true professional, she'd put personal feelings aside to analyze the evening. She'd make one helluva surfer, bouncing back from the biggest dumps. Sharp, too.

Feeling unaccountably lighter, he laughed. "You know, I've been wondering the same thing myself. Probably a bit of both. He's a complicated bastard."

"I gather the two of you don't see eye to eye."

"Nope. He's never forgiven me for getting expelled."

She cocked her head. "You were expelled? What for?"

"Taking dope to school."

"Ah, so you wanted to get expelled."

He was taken aback. "No." Then he thought about it and realized that, subconsciously, he probably had. "Maybe." Strange he'd never really thought of it like that before.

She leaned against the door to look at him more clearly in the darkness. "Why?"

He was silent for a second. "I guess I didn't want to follow in the footsteps laid out in front of me. Dad had been top of his class, and so had Rob." Jake shrugged. "It really pisses the old man off to have a failure of a son."

"You aren't a failure. You're a world-class surfer."

"He'd rather I was a world-class financier."

"Mmm, I can see that."

Silence fell again, but this time it felt companionable. He could detect a faint hint of her perfume through the smell of diesel.

"So this Jungle Paradise Resort—c'mon, Sass, you can't really think it's a good idea."

She didn't answer immediately. Her voice, as

ever, was soft and reasonable, when she said, "Not the Mayan ruin part, no. Kurt went slightly overboard there."

"Slightly?"

She laughed. "Okay, a lot. He's cut from the same cloth as Andy."

"Yeah. Whangarimu World. How did Andy come up with that lemon?" Jake shook his head. "I'd like to say the guy's on drugs, but no. Seriously, though, are all your resorts as crass as that?"

"Not at all. Polynesian Paradise in Hawaii is lovely, all rock pools and waterfalls. A touch clichéd if you like, but very nice to stay at. The one in Mexico has a lot of panache and the Italian one is stunning. But you know how it goes. There was always a demand for the new, the never-thought-of. That was when they started to become extravaganzas and we got a reputation for it. Like the Olympics, the pressure is on for each one to outclass the one before."

"In tastelessness?"

But she would not be drawn. "In meeting customer preference."

Jake snorted. "You'd stuff up all of this for customer preference?" He gestured to the still harbor waters embossed in moonlight. The intricate silhouettes of gnarled pohutukawa flew past as he swung the Jeep down the driveway and pulled up in front of the house. As he switched off the engine and killed the lights, they could hear the haunting notes of the morepork.

"Listen to that owl," he said. "Who will hear that over the din of casinos and discos?"

"Who hears it now," she replied softly, "apart from you and the boys?"

Caught off guard, he didn't know how to reply. He wasn't about to concede the point, but couldn't refute it, either.

Her perfume remained tantalizingly faint. He leaned closer, ignoring the tug of his seat belt pulling him back.

"I didn't mean it personally," he said, looking into the dark hollows of her eyes, and this time knew it was the truth.

"It was a good speech you gave."

Her voice conjured images of feminine dresses from the thirties and couples making out on American porch swings.

"Thanks. Did it convince you?"

She chuckled. "Great oratory doesn't mean you're necessarily right. Look at Hitler."

Was she also leaning in just that much closer?

"Yeah, you're right. Look at lawyers."

As she laughed again, he couldn't resist. He reached out and tucked that fallen strand of hair behind her ear. It was like silk. Of course it was. Miss Pain-in-the would make sure every detail of her life was perfect. His hand lingered by her ear. He could so easily draw her to him and—

Her hand came up and clamped his wrist. "We can't."

"No," he agreed, "we can't." But he didn't take his hand away.

"You've got to stop this…" She paused.

"What?" He couldn't help it—he stroked her hair, ignoring her restraining fingers.

"This blowing hot and cold."

He laughed. "It's better than always being so bloody cool and superior."

"Well, it's got to stop." She looked like a schoolteacher chastising a naughty kid, so he dropped a kiss on her nose.

"You've already said that."

"Because you haven't stopped," she pointed out. He noticed, though, that she wasn't pushing him away. "What do you want, Jake?"

"For an overpaid hotshot, you aren't very bright. I thought I was making myself quite clear."

In the moonlight he saw the reproving, sideways glance she threw at him as she let go of his hand and began undoing her seat belt. He leaned back and grinned.

"What? Running scared?"

"No. Running sensible." She must have been flustered. Uncharacteristically, she was fumbling with the buckle.

"Speaking of running, fancy a real run tomorrow morning?"

Her seat belt finally came free. "What's a real run?"

"Outside. Away from your treadmill. Breathe real air for once."

"You are so full of it." She opened her door.

"If you aren't up to it—"

She got out. "See you pronto at six. I don't wait around."

"I know, I know. Time is money." But she had already gone. He was left alone, laughing softly in the darkness. Score one for him.

Except he was the one left with a libido tied in knots.

CHAPTER TWELVE

"MORNING, SASS. Ready for that run?"

Jake's voice, deep and maddeningly cheerful, carried into the sleep-out, where Sass was pulling on running shoes. Damn! She'd hoped he'd be late, so she wouldn't have to face him just yet. It had been a sleepless night with too much to think about, what with the meeting and all. She steered away from thoughts about after the meeting in the Jeep. What was he going to be like this morning? She didn't want things getting intense, just wanted to pretend nothing had happened. And it hadn't, had it?

She went out onto the deck to find Jake doing chin-ups from a tree branch. When he saw her he dropped to the ground and walked over to her, the bounce of wired energy in his step. No wonder this guy didn't drink coffee; his blood carried its own caffeine.

"Glad you could make it. It's a glorious morning."

Glancing up, Sass realized that the dark sky

wasn't just caused by the earliness of the hour. Full-bellied black clouds hung overhead. "It looks like rain."

"Don't worry about it."

"What d'you mean? It's ready to bucket down."

"It won't be a problem. Cross my heart."

She watched him solemnly cross his broad left pec, but still didn't trust the look in those eyes.

"Is that a real promise?"

"A real promise. You can't back out now—I thought we could go up to the pa."

He was dangling the carrot and she knew, donkey that she was, she'd go after it. He knew it, too.

"Okay," she said, "let's go."

Jake was right; it was a glorious morning. The sea was pewter and shafts of early sunlight slanted gold through the iron-gray clouds. The hills were very green against the sullen skies. They jogged up the driveway, their strides well-matched. At the top Jake turned left.

"Hey, I thought we were going to the pa."

"We are, but I thought we could go down the road a bit first. Why, aren't you up to it?"

The cocked eyebrow was deliberately employed to goad her—and succeeded.

"Sure." She lengthened her stride into a sprint.

He laughed and picked up his own pace. It was a really dumb thing to do. She hadn't exerted herself beyond a sensible jog in years but there was something about the dirt road stretching out in front of her that reminded her of when she'd been one of her school's long-distance runners.

They flew down the road almost shoulder to shoulder. Suddenly she felt a splash of rain on her nose, another on her head. Then the cloud burst like an overfilled water balloon. They were drenched in seconds.

"You said," she cried accusingly, between breaths, "it wouldn't rain!"

"No," he retorted, "I said it wouldn't be a problem. It's not just lawyers who can play silly buggers with the fine print."

"Oh, man!" But she laughed despite herself. "Can I point out, though, that I'm soaked? That's a problem."

"But is it really?" He glanced her way and she saw his expression was teasing, not triumphant as she'd expected.

The rain was warm as it ran down her face and made her clothes cling to her. But at the same time there was something wonderfully free about getting wet, letting it happen. Enjoying it. "I guess not."

In fact, this surrender to the elements made her feel like a child again and, laughing, she opened her mouth and tried to catch some of the drops.

They'd slowed to a jog again and went as far as

the next bay, watching how the rain rippled and pitted the harbor waters in a world of muted grays and greens. Then a lance of sunlight sliced across their path.

"Sun shower!" cried Jake.

"I haven't seen one of those in years."

"You must get them in New York?"

She shrugged. "I'm indoors a good ninety percent of my life, and of the other ten percent, most of that is early in the morning or late at night."

"It's not much of a life."

She threw him a look. "Hey, watch it, buddy. It's my life and I enjoy it, okay?"

"Okay."

They began running back, and while she'd rather choke than admit it out loud, it sure beat the old treadmill. The rain stopped as suddenly as it had started, and rays of sun pierced the shredded clouds. As Jake and she made their way to the pa̲, a rainbow encircled the peninsula, one foot resting in the waves, the other in Aroha Bay.

"My God, that's beautiful."

"Yeah, we've got the best rainbows in the world because we get so much sun and rain. Sometimes even double ones."

"Really?" The idea enchanted her. "I hope I see one before I go home."

"They're special," he said. "You have to earn them."

"Yeah, yeah."

By the time they reached the pa, the sun was surprisingly warm. The grass and trees steamed around them as they stood on the crest of the small hill. Sass was usually meticulous about warm-up and cool-down stretches. Having failed to do the former, she was determined not to skip the latter. Jake propped against a tree and watched as she began doing side bends.

"So tell me about the pa." She swept one hand over her head and leaned, reaching as far out as she could, then straightened, doing the same on the other side. She wasn't going to let on that she'd already done a considerable amount of research on the topic.

Jake indicated the terraces banding the hillside. "Those were defenses. The Maori perfected trench warfare long before it was introduced in Europe. They threw up stockades and dug trenches to ward off enemy attacks."

"Who attacked? The English?" She leaned over to touch her toes and felt his eyes go to her butt.

"Well, later, yes. But the Maori have always been warriors and fought each other, too. They were legendary fighters. Early explorers were terrified of them."

Feeling nicely stretched, Sass perched on a nearby rock and stared at the hill. It was swathed in a gauzy veil of raindrops, which glinted, bright as diamonds, on the brilliant green grass. She recalled Manu's face from the night before, with his strongly defined bones. "I can imagine." And again she felt glad to have the man on her side.

Jake pulled his T-shirt off, then came to sit at right angles to her on the rock. She could feel his warmth down the left side of her body. If she leaned back just an inch, they'd be touching.

"I hate clinging clothes," he said, "on myself, that is." He glanced over his shoulder and his eyes dropped briefly to the T-shirt plastered to her body. "Feel free to strip off, too."

"No, thanks. One porn star is enough for any pa."

He laughed and she lifted her shirt away from her body, shaking it. "So what did the Maori fight about?"

"The usual. Land, power. Much like last night's meeting, in fact."

Sass refused to take the bait, and changed the subject instead. "So where did the name come from?" She stretched her legs out, flexing her feet.

"What name?" She saw Jake's eyes travel down her legs, then up again.

"Aroha Bay."

"Oh, yeah. Right."

He was clearly distracted and she suppressed a smile. "Well, it comes from a myth about two young lovers from warring tribes—all very Romeo and Juliet. It ended up with them both drowning."

"That's so sad." For a minute Sass stared out over the ocean. It was beautiful and romantic, the perfect setting for a love story. For star-crossed lovers. She gave herself a shake. "A myth, did you say?"

"Yeah, though it's probably based on truth. A lot of the Maori stories were."

"I see."

And she did. Sass fancied she could feel the whisper of lovers' vows in the soft wind, the sighs of lost love in the wash of the waves.

"Seems real on a morning like this, doesn't it?" said Jake, and she turned her head sharply. His green eyes met hers and he laughed self-consciously. "You won't believe this, but I sometimes feel their ghosts at dawn or twilight, when I'm paddling out."

The hairs on her arms rose, but Jake, seeing this, drew different conclusions. "You're cold. We should head back. Besides, my butt's going to sleep on this rock."

He stood up, and Sass did indeed suddenly feel

cold without the solid warmth of his back so close to hers. He put out a hand to pull her up and, as she rose, she flashed back to four days ago, when he'd pulled her to her feet at paintball. His broad, tanned chest was suddenly very close. He tugged her closer, but she quickly slapped her palm against one solid pec. Under her fingers, she could feel his nipple tighten.

"No, Jake. I made myself clear last night."

"Yeah. Well, I didn't get much sleep, so got to thinking. This attraction is in the way, sidetracking us, so we should just sleep together and get it out of our systems."

She rolled her eyes. "That's such a male solution to the problem."

He grinned. "What? Practical and pleasurable?"

"No. Really *dumb.* I've told you already, I don't mix business with pleasure."

"And is this pleasure?" His voice was very soft, very low.

"Yeah, though it burns my butt to admit it."

He still didn't move, either closer or farther away. She should take her hand from his chest, but it seemed to have fused to his body. She could feel the strong beat of his heart, and her own seemed to falter, then fall in with his rhythm.

"We can't keep pretending it isn't there."

"That doesn't mean we have to act on it."

"Too late."

"That was a mistake, like I said at the time. We can't complicate things."

"Again, too late. It's already complicated."

She found the strength to pull her hand away, step back from him. "We can't complicate them any further, then. It wouldn't work, don't you see. Men pretend they like to play the field, but they always get possessive in the end. You'll end up confusing personal issues with the resort discussions."

Jake balled up his T-shirt. "Look, Sass, I can understand blokes getting possessive over you, but frankly, lawyers aren't my type. If you can separate business and relationships, let me assure you, so can I. It's simply that I haven't had sex for twelve months and here you are, an attractive female living in my house and distracting the hell out of me. It's nothing more than that."

"A *year?* Are you kidding me?"

"No."

Sass took another step back and planted her hands on her hips. "How come?"

Under her scrutiny his face flushed, but he tried to shrug it off. "It's nothing."

She thought of Alison and knew there was no way celibacy had been foisted upon him. "On the contrary, it's pertinent to this conversation. Why?"

Jake ran a hand through his damp curls. "I didn't like the person I was a year ago, so decided to change everything. I'd also been accused of having commitment issues so…no more casual sex."

"Then what the hell are you offering me now?"

He laughed. "A respite from your rules and mine! There's an attraction, but as we both know, it'll never go anywhere. So we can kick back and enjoy it for the brief time you're here."

Everything in her brain screamed *Warning!* Every other part of her body thought Jake Finlayson was offering a perfectly reasonable deal. Strange, though, how she'd flinched when he'd said it would never go anywhere, when of course she didn't want it to.

"No, it wouldn't work. You macho guys are always the ones who become the most possessive."

"In my experience it's the woman."

Sass shrugged as she began walking back along the path. "You must go for clingy sorts," she said over her shoulder. "I'm not at all like that."

In two strides Jake was beside her, grabbing her arm and spinning her around. His face very close, his eyes filling her field of vision. "Afraid?"

Somehow she found the strength to pull out of his grasp instead of leaning into him. "No, I'm not *afraid!*" she said, but even as she spoke, she felt an unexpected sliver of fear. "It would just be a really dumb thing to do."

"C'mon, Sass." He moved closer still, his voice soft and wheedling. "The attraction between us isn't going to go away. The more you resist it, the bigger deal it will become. Whereas if we just go with it…" He shrugged eloquently.

She was tempted, she really was, but couldn't let him know that. "Nice try, surf boy, but it's simply not going to happen."

Jake pressed his finger to her lips. His voice, still soft, was very, very sure. "Don't you believe that, Miss Pain-in-the, don't you believe that at all."

CHAPTER THIRTEEN

FOR THE NEXT COUPLE of days Sass made sure she was never alone with Jake. It wasn't difficult, for the days were very busy as she met with all the different interest groups to get her head around the issues. Jake was pretty busy, too, always off in one direction or another. Of course, they had to see each other in the evenings as, true to her word, Sass took over the cooking, much to the boys' noisy appreciation. She enjoyed chatting with them when they came home from school, and couldn't stop herself from checking on their progress with assignments. Her close interest acted as the spur she hoped it would, and they did knuckle down more to their studies—except for Brad. He was charming but slippery when it came to evading schoolwork.

After dinner it was fun to kick back with the guys to watch a movie or play video games. She couldn't do the racing games, but found she had quite a talent for Guitar Hero. This minor success gave her a peculiarly warm glow.

During this time, Jake never once made a move on her. Had probably thought better of it, she decided. *Good.* She was acutely aware of him whenever he walked into the room, even felt she could somehow sense him a second before he arrived. But he gave no sign he was similarly attuned to her. Neither he nor the boys could resist giving her a hard time about her American ways. She didn't mind. Quite the contrary, it made her feel part of the family. Not that they were a family as such, but somehow Jake made them seem as if they were.

Sass was in a good mood when she drove into Whangarimu on Friday morning to meet with the ABORD group. At the town meeting, Manu had impressed her with his intelligence and humanity, and today he'd brought along supporters with their own stories and reasons for being pro-development.

"It's about jobs," explained Eloise, a woman in her forties in a twinset and faux pearls. "We have one of the highest unemployment rates in the country." Her eyes dropped to her clasped hands as she added, "My husband killed himself after twenty months' unemployment."

Everyone fell silent, digesting what she'd told them.

"If the country doesn't want me to be a dole bludger," Neill, a pimply young man, finally said, "then it needs to give me a job. I've never had a real one."

Sass could see his belligerence stemmed from deep-seated frustration, and remembered, with a stab, the same sullenness in her brothers.

Dorothy, at least seventy and a startling sight with bright purple bangs, nodded. "We're losing too many young people. We need to use what we've got—and that's scenery." She tapped the tabletop with one purple-tipped finger to make her point.

"We've seen what the tourist dollar has done for Rotorua," Manu continued, "and we'd like to bring some of that cash up here. Give our young folks opportunities."

"And with the tourists coming in," Dorothy added, "our arts community will do better. We've a lot of artists living here but there's no one to buy our work."

At the end of the meeting Manu clasped Sass's hand in his. "It's been a pleasure meeting with you," he said sincerely. "You're not at all what we were expecting. We really appreciate the way you've listened to us. However—" he looked directly at her "—you haven't said whether you'll support us when the time comes."

Sass looked straight back at him. "Manu, I'm really glad to have heard ABORD's point of view, but I'm still collecting all the facts. Obviously, my company is keen to make the resort work. I will not publicize my recommendations yet because it's up to Paradise Resorts to make the final decision, but please know I will make every effort to evaluate the situation objectively and not be swayed by any one individual or group."

Manu smiled. "That's some comfort. Jake Finlayson can be very persuasive."

For a brief, appalling moment, Sass remembered their kiss so vividly she could almost feel his lips on hers. She laughed lightly. "Don't you worry at all about Jake Finlayson." Her voice was strong and confident enough to fool anyone. She almost bought it herself. Looking around at the committee, she added, "I've so enjoyed meeting y'all today. Please believe me when I say that I'll do my utmost to find a win-win solution."

At that, they all burst out laughing.

"Win-win, that's a good one," Dorothy said.

"Fat chance!" Neill declared.

"Oh, dear," said Eloise, but when she wiped her eyes, it was to mop up tears of laughter.

Manu leaned forward and kissed her cheek. "I promise you, Sass, that if you find a win-win for this, we'll invite you back to run for mayor."

SASS HAD AGREED TO MEET Jake at Rob and Moana's after her meeting, to discuss the party they'd all been invited to Saturday night. As she drove through the streets, which even in this short time were beginning to look familiar, she thought about ABORD and was filled with a sense of purpose. She could help them, help the community. This was what she loved about her job. The resorts not only provided holidays, but also jobs. It was sad about the terns, but they were only talking seven birds here. And as for Jake and his preposterous propositions—well, he could just forget it. She wasn't some teenager, slave to her hormones. She was a rational, intelligent woman.

She pulled up behind Jake's beat-up Jeep and got out of the car. There was a high mechanical whining in the air, but she paid it little attention as she looked at the two vehicles. Her small car seemed jaunty and shiny and well, yes, sassy, behind Jake's rugged monster, covered in dust and dings.

Briskly, she clipped up the garden path in the high heels she'd succumbed to that morning, having missed elegance these past few days, and knocked on the front door with three sharp raps.

Moana opened the door, Jacob perched on one hip, and Sass could now clearly hear the screaming buzz of machinery.

"Hey, Moana, what's going on?"

"Sass, come in. The men have brought down the old pine and are chainsawing it into firewood." She waggled her eyebrows. "Want to see muscle in motion? It's quite a sight."

Sass laughed and followed Moana through the house and onto the back porch. There in the garden was a toppled tree, now mostly dissected into logs. Jake, with a safety helmet jammed over his curls, was wielding a chainsaw with controlled, graceful movements while Rob cleared the severed tree limbs. Their steps seemed almost choreographed as they moved together in unspoken understanding. The smells of wood chips and machine exhaust filled the air.

"They're nearly there!" shouted Moana. "Just as well. It's a pretty sight but the noise is awful."

"Jacob doesn't seem worried about it!" Sass shouted back, stroking the baby's head as he watched the action, fascinated.

"Chainsawing is hardwired into the Finlayson psyche. Matt had them out cutting wood almost before they could walk. Oh, good, looks like they're finishing. We can stay outside now and enjoy the sun."

But even as she said it, the phone inside rang and, grimacing in apology, Moana disappeared inside. Sass perched on the steps of the deck and watched as, after the final branches came free, the brothers straightened and Jake switched off his saw. The sudden silence seemed to heighten all

Sass's other senses. Jake laid his chainsaw on the ground, then unbuckled his chaps to reveal board-shorts underneath. Both brothers threw off their helmets, rubbing their heads. Next the T-shirts were pulled off to reveal tanned backs glistening with perspiration, and they stretched to ease their shoulders and back muscles. Both were lean, but Jake had a surfer's powerful shoulders and biceps, thighs packed with muscle.

Rationally, Sass knew feminine appreciation of raw masculinity was nothing more than DNA left over from the Stone Age. Rationally, she acknowledged that this quicksilver excitement was little more than a prerecorded response to a certain stimulus. Rationally, she knew she was a sports car and he was nothing more than a beat-up Jeep. But just as rationally, she could suddenly see some of the beauty of his logic. If it were all nothing more than DNA sequencing, why then…

Jake turned, wiping his forehead with his arm, and saw Sass. "Hey," he said, sauntering over with a smile that made her heart skip. "How long have you been here?"

"Just arrived. Quite a grizzly sight, considering you're supposed to be conservationists."

"Looks bad, I know," Rob said, a step behind Jake, "but there were extenuating circumstances, Your Honor." He leaned down and dropped a light, sweaty kiss on her cheek. "It was bound to come down in the next big storm. Good to see you. All ready for the *Grease* party tomorrow night?"

"A *Grease* party? Is that what it is? You're kidding me, right? Didn't they go out of fashion in, like, 1979?"

Rob looked at Jake with a wounded expression. "Ms. Walker here thinks we're hokey."

Jake shook his head. "Don't be hard on the kid. She's fresh from New York. What does she know about the latest trends? America hasn't even had a female president yet. We probably shouldn't mention taking the America's Cup off them, either."

His curls were matted and rivulets of sweat ran down his temples. He smelled of machine oil and testosterone. The chainsaw was switched off but the air was still charged.

"Yeah, yeah. One little yacht race and you guys think you can take on all of the U.S. of A. A touch of the small man's syndrome if you ask me."

"Hey, nothing small about the Finlaysons," said Rob. "Well, me and Jacob at any rate. Can't speak for Jake." He ducked as his brother swung a punch. "If you'll excuse me, Sass, I'll go shower."

He disappeared into the house just as Moana came out, carrying a can of beer. "Here you go, payment for the worker."

Jake cracked it open and took a long pull. Sass couldn't help looking at the long lines of his throat. "Man, that's good," he said.

Privately, she agreed. Then remembering that she was supposed to be brisk, she turned to Moana. "I've just been hearing about the *Grease* party tomorrow night. Are we expected to dress up?"

"Don't worry about it—I've got it covered. Here, take Jacob, will you? And I'll get the coffee on."

She held her son out to Sass, who raised her hands in surrender as if the baby were a time bomb.

"Whoa, I don't do kids, thanks all the same."

"Don't be silly." Moana dropped Jacob into Sass's lap, forcing her to catch him. "There's nothing to it."

Sass looked down at the little boy. She hadn't been this close to a baby in years. Gingerly, she scooped him up, and as she inhaled that distinctive baby smell, she remembered being five and seeing her brother Adam for the first time. "Hey, buddy." Jacob regarded her with steadfast black eyes. "Had a good sleep?"

What to say to babies? She wasn't going to start with the baby talk, so she jigged her knee up and down. Jacob looked interested. She jigged again and he giggled.

Jake plopped down on the step beside her and

leaned against the railing as he held the can, beaded in moisture, to his brow. He was covered in fine sawdust and the hair on his chest glowed gold in the sun. She crossed her legs, grasped Jacob's plump little hands and wrists and started a brisk trotting rhythm. Jacob shrieked with laugher, which made her smile. "You'd do well in the rodeo, kid."

"Rodeo?" Jake regarded her quizzically. "I suppose they're a compulsory part of a Texan upbringing."

"Not necessarily, but in my case, yes, when I was younger. My dad's on the circuit."

Jake looked impressed. "He's a rider?"

Sass hesitated. "Sort of."

"What do you mean, sort of?"

She bit her lip. "He's one of the clowns."

Kids at school had died laughing at that one. She never talked about it at all in New York.

Jake's eyes lit up. "Yeah? He must have balls."

"I don't know about that," she said. "He sure lacked stamina in the family department."

Sass regretted saying it the minute it slipped out, and to cover her embarrassment, she buried her face in Jacob's stomach, blowing raspberries. The baby shrieked with laughter again and clutched her hair. She gently pried open his tiny hands to inspect the minute perfection of his plump palms and fingers, then pretended to nibble them. When she looked up, Jake was watching her. "What?"

He smiled his slow, surf smile and despite her resolve, her insides liquefied. "You're great with babies."

"Yeah, well, this one's a little heart-warmer."

Jake stretched out his long legs and leaned his head back on the railing behind him. He was feline in the way he could look both completely relaxed and entirely alert. The sun caught the side of his face, accentuating the high cheeks, the jaw that could set so pugnaciously.

"If your father was a rodeo clown and your mother was an English teacher, how the hell did they get together in the first place?"

By leaning back, he'd created distance between them, which helped. She hated deep-and-meaning-fuls, especially when the guy leaned forward to stare into her eyes.

"They met at a party my dad and some of his friends crashed. She was pretty and had class, and he was handsome and wild. It was just a fling until I happened along."

Sass ran a finger down Jacob's forehead and nose to his mouth, and let him nip on it. Jake sat motionless. She wasn't used to people sitting so still. In New York everyone was like her, revved on coffee and stress. Jake, however, was used to harnessing his energy and patience while waiting on his board. Then, when the right wave came, he unleashed it all in one crazy, adrenaline-pumping, death-defying ride.

"And then?" he prompted, taking another sip of his beer.

She shrugged. "They married and Mom went on teaching. She just loves poetry. But Dad couldn't settle. Was always off to rodeos all over the place—roping heifers in and out of the arena, from all accounts. His stints away became longer than his stints at home, and the arguing increased. He left for good when I was twelve."

Jake grimaced. "Tough. How did your mum cope? You said the other night your dad left debts."

Sass looked out over the garden with its flower beds and fence and pile of firewood in the far corner, ready for winter nights. A tire was tied to the branch of a tree. She'd had a swing just like it in their yard. For the first time she realized how her mother must have felt, selling their home—and all her dreams of happily-ever-after—to move into a trailer park.

Sass looked back at Jake. "She started drinking."

She waited, half-defiant, for his response—this golden surfer boy with his rich family. At the same time, the lawyer in her was questioning why she'd chosen this moment to expose her secret shames to this particular man. Was it the need to drive a wedge into the dangerous connection developing between them? More worrisome still, was it because she was testing him?

"Poor lady. Hard on you kids, too."

"It wasn't like, you know, trailer-trash drinking. She's a functioning alcoholic. No one ever guessed."

Jake nodded. "My grandfather was an alcoholic. I understand how it is. Nice person but hell to live with."

To hide tears that suddenly threatened, Sass cuddled Jacob close. He felt so good. She was never going to have babies—they didn't figure in her game plan—but at this moment she got why women went mushy over the idea.

"It wasn't all Dad's fault," she said abruptly. She didn't know why she had this need to defend her father, but it seemed important, somehow, that Jake got the full picture. "Mom also had a fling—with a Cherokee. Adam was her papoose, but Daddy raised him exactly the same as Cole and me."

"Deep down, he sounds like a good man, Sass."

"Yeah, I think he is," she said. She'd never discussed her father with anyone before. Jake's nonjudgmental attitude made it easier. "For years

I just hated him, but more recently I've given it a lot of thought and realize he's just…kind of weak, I guess."

Unable to hold the intensity of Jake's gaze anymore, she glanced away with a laugh. "You should've seen us together—my fair-haired mom, two blondies, and then this dark Cherokee kid—the best looking of us all."

At that moment Moana came out, carrying a tray. "You've got a Native American for a brother? That's so cool!"

Sass looked at her with genuine affection. "Adam would be so pleased to hear that. He's always had a complex, being the odd one out."

"Oh, we're all mixed blood in New Zealand. Take me. I'm Maori, but also Irish and a touch of French." She handed a coffee to Sass. "Jake and Rob, on the other hand, are English and Dally, with only a smattering of Maori."

"Do you guys ever speak real English? What's Dally?"

Jake crumpled his beer can. "Dalmations. A lot came out at the turn of the century."

"That's where he gets his beautiful green eyes." Moana sighed. "Rob was short-changed and got brown like me. I'd hoped that Jacob would get them, but no, he's going to be the same as the rest of the whanau."

"Whanau?"

"Extended family." Rob arrived with a plate of steaming muffins. "Here, hot from the oven. Tuck in."

"How do you do it?" Sass demanded.

"What?" Moana asked.

"How do you have a kid, a job, a home and still have time for baking?"

Moana laughed. "Family secret, sorry. I'd tell you but then I'd have to kill you. You okay with Jacob?"

"Absolutely, he's my hostage. You don't get him back until you explain how to be All Things Woman."

"Oh, all right. Aunt Betty." Moana sat back and grinned enigmatically.

Rob laughed and Sass looked at Jake. "I don't get it."

He took pity on her. "Betty Crocker muffin mix."

"Really? Oh, man. I feel so taken in."

"Yeah," Moana said, holding out her arms, "but whatever works, right? Now pay up, and give me my baby."

"Gladly," said Sass, handing Jacob over. "I couldn't work out why he was suddenly concentrating so hard."

Moana wrinkled her nose and, without pausing,

passed the infant straight on to his father. “Your turn.”

Rob groaned, but Moana said bracingly, “It gets better. You and Jake are holding the fort and the infant for the next few hours. Sass and I are going *Grease* shopping.”

CHAPTER FOURTEEN

THEY TOOK SASS'S CAR.

"I wanna be flash for a change," Moana said. But the sports car looked incongruous reflected in the dusty windows of the secondhand clothes shop they drew up in front of.

"Are you sure about this?" Sass asked, eyeing the peeling paint on the shop frontage.

"Trust me," she said, "this shop is pure vintage. Things here haven't sold in over twenty years."

Self-conscious in her noisy high heels, Sass followed Moana into the shop, which smelled so musty she paused in the doorway. Unwanted memories of shopping in places exactly like this surfaced. Revulsion welled in her, but Moana was already holding up shiny, leopard-print Lycra leggings and waggling her splendidly arched eyebrows suggestively.

"How about these little passion-pants, then?"

"Oh my God, some of the women in the trailer park used to sit around smoking in things like that."

Moana laughed. "They're your size, girlfriend. We'll put them to one side for you. They're only two bucks. Come on, you check out that lot over there."

Sass went gingerly over to the rack, but as she began sorting through the clothes, she got a grip on herself. After all, she wasn't the poor kid on the block anymore. She was Sass Walker, NY lawyer. What had happened to her *then* wasn't about to affect her *now.* Denial had always been her strongest weapon, but today she was discovering that confronting memories was easier than she'd expected.

As she relaxed, Sass found herself getting into the swing of the treasure hunt, and by the end of the afternoon she and Moana had two overflowing bags of "possibilities" and felt they'd earned a coffee. At a small café down at the marina, they sat outside and admired the yachts reflected in the afternoon high tide.

"So," said Moana, skimming off a teaspoon of cappuccino froth and savoring it, "you and Jake seem to be getting on."

Her tone was casual, but Sass wasn't deceived. "Yeah, seems so," was all she'd offer.

"He's a nice guy. Mind you, I'm partial to the Finlayson boys. Do you have anyone back in New York?"

Sass laughed and shook her head. "Moana, you'd be a hopeless witness. Your lines of thought are far too transparent."

Moana smiled, unabashed. "I don't hedge around."

"I've noticed."

"And I've noticed you haven't answered the question. So, do you have a boyfriend back home?"

Sass looked away, over at the yachts. A man was rowing a dinghy back to a boat with a Canadian flag. His T-shirt was stretched and faded. In New York, people would be wearing boots and long coats right now, battling winter sleet.

"No, there's no one."

"How come? A gorgeous woman like you? I'd have thought you'd have them all panting at your feet."

Sass blushed. Deep down she couldn't believe that other people couldn't see the gangly trailer kid she was. To cover up her embarrassment, she shrugged and sat back in her chair, cradling her cup.

"There's not really time for relationships in my life. I'm pretty committed to my job." She saw Moana's expression and smiled. "Yeah, I know you guys think what I do is reprehensible, but that's not the way I see it. We go in, take unused land and build resorts for ordinary families to have their week in paradise. It's easy for you guys to scorn development. You live in exquisite surroundings. But if you lived in some boring old town in the back of beyond, let me tell you, you'd be hanging out for a holiday in Paradise Mexico, too. We provide an escape for people, a chance to live the fantasy for just a week or two."

"And make a killing in the process." Moana's tone was dry, and Sass inclined her head in acknowledgment. "Mind you," Moana continued, "when you put it like that, it doesn't sound that bad. But getting back on topic, Rob and I had full-time jobs and yet we still found time for a relationship. Even New York lawyers must get together and procreate, or the species would die out."

Sass laughed. "That's the problem. I'm not interested in procreating. There've been some nice guys, but they all had picket fences in their eyes. Living in a bedroom community with two point four kids doesn't hold any appeal."

Moana nodded thoughtfully and tucked a strand of her long black hair behind her ear. "Well, that makes sense. But it sounds lonely."

"I'm not *lonely*." That sounded sharper than she intended.

"Sorry, Sass, I shouldn't have said that."

But the woman was a psychologist and Sass knew her reaction had just been filed away in Moana's mind. Sass decided to move the conversation away from herself, not wanting further analysis. "What about Jake? How come he doesn't have any girlfriends?"

Damn! Talk about trains of thought… But Moana gave no sign that she'd noticed. She was as professional at her job as Sass was at hers. Instead, she shrugged.

"It's strange, I've known both brothers since they were teenagers, and this past year has been the only time I haven't seen Jake with half a dozen girls hanging around him. There are women here pining for him to show a flicker of interest, but so far he seems to remain oblivious."

"And before now? No serious relationships?"

Moana leaned back in her chair and gave Sass a long look. "Jake's as cagey as you when it comes to talking about personal things. Generally Kiwi blokes aren't very good at sharing their feelings—there's this whole Man Alone thing that's part of their male psyche. Not surprising, really. The Pakeha—that's the Europeans—had it tough when they first came to New Zealand. It seems tame now, with fields and sheep, but it used to be impenetrably dense forests, flooding rivers and thousands of miles of loneliness. They turned in on themselves, built small huts in the wilderness and hunkered down. Self-reliant and alone."

Sass blinked. "Wow. That's quite a picture."

Moana smiled smugly. "I wrote a paper for a pysch journal explaining the problems we have with our boys."

"I see. Enter Brad and Company."

"Exactly. I think it also goes some way to explain the Kiwi laconic understatement. For example, if a guy is over-the-moon-thrilled-to-his-socks excited, he'll say, 'That's cool' in a quiet way. If he really likes the look of something or if he's enjoyed himself, he says, 'Yeah, not bad.' The shittiest day becomes 'not the best.' So if one ever says, 'I quite like you,' it that means you are the hottest babe he's fancied in a long time and he could well be on the way to love."

Sass laughed. "In New York, everything's amped up."

"There's one exception, though. *Sport.* Then Kiwi males yell and hurl abuse. On the field they slap each other on the back, and players can even hug each other in a rough sort of way."

"Now that behavior I do recognize. It's a Y-chromosome thing, I guess."

"Yeah. As for Jake, he was involved with some girl in Hawaii. If you can get him to talk about it, you're a better counselor than I. He won't give anything away if he doesn't want to. Just like you."

"As a psychologist, you should realize there's no way anything can happen between me and Jake if we're both so cold and repressed."

"I didn't say you were cold. Actually, I wouldn't say that about either of you. I simply said you didn't give things away."

"If opposites attract, and we are two of a kind, wipe that look off your face."

Moana grinned. "Don't worry. I think there are more than enough opposites between the two of you to keep you sparking a long, long time. Look, tomorrow night, why don't you and Jake come for dinner? Then we can get ready together. It'll be fun—we can pretend we're teenagers again."

Sass groaned. "A *Grease* party is more like a bad dream from my childhood, but yeah, dinner would be great."

CHAPTER FIFTEEN

JAKE WOKE SASS EARLY on Saturday morning.

"The westerlies have kicked in," he said, clearly excited. "It's really going off at Shippies, so the boys and I are driving up. Want to come?"

Shaking her head, Sass struggled to her elbows. "Shippies? What time is it?"

"Five o'clock. Shippies—Shipwreck Bay—is a few hours drive north of here, on the West Coast. C'mon, you have to come. It has the longest left-hand break in the world."

She couldn't help laughing. "Irresistible as that is, I sadly have to decline your lovely invitation. I've got work to do."

"It's Saturday!"

"Yeah, and I have a report to write. No," she said as his eyes narrowed, "I haven't decided anything yet. But I can make a start on it."

"Damn right you haven't decided anything yet. You've still got to meet the terns. I'd meant to take you today, but—"

"Yeah, I know, the westerlies. Go on, go. Enjoy."

"Will do." Taking her completely by surprise, Jake dropped a kiss on the top of her head. "Don't work too hard," he ordered, before bounding out of the room and clattering down the steps. Sass stared after him. She couldn't read anything into it, it was just an impulsive gesture born out of high spirits. Nevertheless, for the rest of the day, as she labored over the report, the memory made her smile.

The guys returned in the early evening, tired but exhilarated. Almost immediately, she and Jake left to have dinner with Moana and Rob before the party.

Never having had a sister, Sass hadn't known what fun it was to get ready for a party with someone else. She laughed harder than she had in years. Somehow, Moana coerced her into the leopard-print leggings and a black T-shirt so tight her lungs felt constricted. They'd found teeteringly high, wooden heels, and she'd even been persuaded into letting Moana use heated curlers and do her hair in a semblance of the Olivia curly-top style. A vinyl black jacket, all zips and silver studs, completed the ensemble.

"You look *fantastic.*" Moana stepped back to admire the effect. "Man, I'm good! You look like a babe."

Sass laughed. "I feel like a hooker. I'm sure I'm going to break my ankle on these things."

"Get over it. You'll steal the show."

"I doubt that. You're looking pretty hot yourself."

Moana twisted to study her rear end in the mirror. "Not bad, but I wish I'd shed my baby fat. My backside seems enormous in these jeans. Oh, well, Rob vowed for better or worse, so he's stuck with me now."

"I think he'll come to terms with the idea."

In fact, Moana was stunning in skintight Levi's. Her "baby fat" accentuated her curves. She wore a blood-red, off-the-shoulders shiny top, and her black hair fell to her hips. She, too, was wobbling on heels far higher than anything she normally wore.

"What I don't understand," she said, "is why our mothers weren't all crippled. These things are death traps. Let's see what the guys have come up with."

As they walked in, the brothers, who'd been sprawled in front of the TV watching sports, got to their feet.

"Nice outfits," Rob said.

"Drop-dead gorgeous," Moana mouthed to Sass.

But Sass didn't need a translation. Jake was taking her in from head to toe. Then he took her in again, lingering this time. She had no trouble interpreting the nod and the quick indrawn breath.

"Looking good," he said.

Moana rolled her eyes and gave Sass the I-told-you look. "Yeah, well, you two have scrubbed up okay, too."

So women could also use the laconic understatement, Sass realized. The guys hadn't done much—both wore jeans and white T-shirts—but there was something swaggering in their manner that was pure Travolta. Maybe it was the big boots, but either could have posed as the Marlboro man.

Moana wasn't completely satisfied, though. "You can't go dressed the same. Come over here, Jake."

He walked up to her suspiciously. She snatched up a large pair of scissors.

"What the—oi, that's my T-shirt, crazy lady!" But it was too late. She'd already snipped off one sleeve and was hacking at the other. "Attack your husband, not me!"

She shook her head. "First off, I'm not having him strut about and become the target of all the lecherous women of Whangarimu. Secondly, he hasn't got your biceps."

"Hey." Rob protested.

"It's all right, babe," Moana explained, "I love you for your brains and personality."

"Thank you very much," he retorted, insulted.

"There." She stepped back and surveyed her handiwork. "Whaddya think, Sass?"

Sass tilted her head and sized him up, starting

at his battered Doc Martens and traveling slowly up those long legs, noting the way the denim tightened a fraction on the thighs and molded to his butt. Her eyes moved slowly up the T-shirt that strained over the chest, and she nodded approvingly at the way the ragged edges of the sleeve holes drew attention to the bronzed arms, allowing a glimpse of honed muscles running across his shoulders. This guy was *ripped.* She looked into his face. He seemed half amused, half annoyed by her appraisal.

"Hmm, not bad."

Moana high-fived her. "Gonna have you talking like a native before you leave."

The brothers exchanged glances and shook their heads.

"Totally losing it, but we're stuck with them now. Shall we go?" Rob said, proffering his arm to his wife.

THE PARTY WAS HELD in a country hall outside town. It was more like a glorified barn, Sass thought, with whitewashed wooden walls and wooden floors. A huge mirrored disco ball hung from the ceiling, which was festooned with balloons and streamers. The blaring music was straight from the seventies and took her back to her childhood, listening to her mom and dad—

when he was around—and their friends after she'd gone to bed, playing Fleetwood Mac, Moody Blues, Billy Joel. Oh God, and the Bee Gees, she remembered as *Saturday Night Fever* began blasting out. How could she have forgotten the Bee Gees?

"I'll never survive this," she muttered, and that was her last coherent thought. Alison came racing up in a fifties-style circular skirt and bobby socks, instantly towing Jake off for a dance. He threw Sass an apology over his shoulder, but he didn't need to worry because some guy with the skinniest legs she'd ever seen, in stovepipe jeans, was already asking her to dance.

All ages and types were on the floor dancing… everything; rock and roll, disco and hip-hop. One of Sass's favorite moments was seeing Jake do the twist with a kid about eight years old. When he swung her up in the best rock-and-roll tradition, she was grinning like a jack-o-lantern. Sass danced with Rob, with Moana, and with a whole bunch of guys she'd never met before, but who just kept on coming.

She caught sight of Jake from time to time through the crowds, always dancing with a new girl. But no matter how many times he changed partners, they all seemed to wear the same silly, idolizing smile. Man, he must be feeding them some lines to get *that* reaction. Still, Sass had to admit the guy could dance. His performance of "Greased Lightning" drew an impromptu burst of applause. Sass mentioned this fact to Moana when they finally sat to swig icy beers.

"Those Finlayson boys look okay on the dance floor." She reckoned she was getting the hang of this laconicspeak, and shrugged off the jacket. She'd been shy about the tightness of her T-shirt but was now way too hot to care.

Moana waggled her eyebrows over her bottle. "Yeah, they're good, but you're a pretty mean dancer yourself, Sass. Must be all that barn dancing you grew up with in Texas." As Sass snorted into her beer, Moana glanced at her watch. "Damn, it's midnight. We should be getting back to the babysitter. You okay here alone while I go look for Rob?"

"Sure. Glad of the break. My feet are killing me."

"Ditto. Don't think I'll be able to walk tomorrow."

Moana teetered off as the opening notes for "You're the One That I Want" roused a cheer from the dance floor. Sass groaned. Man, this really was hokey—but fun. A shadow fell over her and when she looked up, there was Jake, his hand outstretched.

"We haven't danced."

A fact hard to refute. The hand hard to reject.

"Okay."

She followed him into the crush in the middle of the hall, his smile as much as his broad shoulders clearing them a path. He had nice manners, a good touch with people. Light and easy. But when he turned, she thought again how he was pure Travolta—in a tawny, surfer way. Deep inside, she located her Olivia and, flinging back her shoulders, for the next few minutes let herself respond to the bad boy Jake was playing. They swung together, rubbed and bumped, laughed and kidded around in the strutting, flirty style of the song. Jake's mop of curls was wilder than ever from the heat, the sweat, the movement, his eyes alight with fun and challenge. He picked her up and swooped her between his legs, then, as if she was no weight at all, tossed her from one side of his waist to the other. The walls of the hall blurred; the only sound was the beat of the music and the silly lyrics with their "oo, hoo hoos."

For the final notes, he picked her up and spun her around and around. When he put her back on her feet, they were breathing heavily, staring at each other.

"And after that lively number," the DJ announced, "all you oldies will need to catch your breaths, so here's a knee-wobbler to take you back."

As Fleetwood Mac's "Oh Daddy" began to play, Jake pulled her into his arms. Sass, out of breath, relaxed against his chest. Even in these shoes, she was still not as tall as he was. That was nice. Swaying with him, she closed her eyes, inhaling the clean tang of his sweat, feeling his heart gradually slow. The hand clasping hers was large but gentle. His other hand was at the small of her back, his thumb moving in caressing circles. It made her want to arch and purr. It made her want to stretch so the caress could go up and down her spine. It made her want to run her own nails up and down that bronze back to feel the muscles flex under her touch.

It made her want.

Sharply, she pulled herself together and raised her head. At her sudden movement, Jake looked down, and in the soft light of the dance floor, his pupils were dilated. It was as if he could see into her and, as if hypnotized, she felt unable to break away. DNA sequencing. Had to be, to make her feel this breathless. This weak. This aching and needy.

Stevie Nick's husky voice came to an end.

"Let's go home," Jake said very softly.

CHAPTER SIXTEEN

LATER SASS COULDN'T remember the drive home, except for the image of Jake's fierce concentration as he whipped along that dark, winding country road at a breathless speed. They didn't talk, didn't touch. The agony of anticipation and arousal was suffocating. And delicious. They hurtled down the bumpy driveway and came to a skidding halt outside her cottage. Somehow they made it up the steps to her room and laughed as they collided with the bed. Then there was the blessed, mindless relief of giving vent to their passion.

The sex was good; great even. The best sex she'd ever had. Jake was the sort of lover every girl dreamed of. First, he had the body—a body that was pure lean strength and muscle. But he was so much more than that. He'd been fun, flirty, gentle and, yes, demanding, too, and she'd been just as demanding back. He'd roused her to almost screaming point before he'd come in a pounding climax. Twice.

They fell back, side by side. She was satiated, but he didn't seem to be in quite the same space.

"Um, Sass?"

"Mmm?" She was so drowsy.

"Sass?" He cleared his throat and tried again. "Sass, did you by any chance, in fact, um, come?"

Her contentment fell away in a flash.

"What do you mean?"

"I just thought—and I could be wrong—that it wasn't, well, for you what it was for me. And if it wasn't, I'm really sorry."

She sat up, gathering the sheet over her breasts, feeling horribly exposed. "Just what do you mean?"

"I don't think I gave you an orgasm."

There it was. He'd said it, and she cursed herself. As a lawyer she knew better than to ask a question she didn't want the answer to.

"Either time," he added. "The first, I know I was quick, but the second, I really thought it was going to happen."

Her worst nightmare had just come true. No guy had ever confronted her about that before. She might have known it would be Jake Wonder-boy Finlayson who'd pinpoint her one failing. Still, she wasn't about to concede anything.

"It was great. One of the best lays I've had. So relax, buddy. Your reputation as surf stud is safe with me."

He drew back to look up at her. "Whoa, hey, there's no reason to fly off like that. It's not me I'm worried about. I'm concerned about you."

"I don't need your concern. I'm fine. Better than fine. I'm great, just *great.*"

"Well, that's okay then."

She glowered at him for a second, then lay down, the sheet still clutched to her chest. "Don't you think you should be getting back to your own bed now?"

Ignoring this dismissal, he rolled onto his side, propped himself up on one elbow and looked down at her. The only light came from the moon, so the planes of his face were rimmed with silver, the hollows of his cheeks dark pools of shadow.

"Come on, Sass. Tell me truthfully. I felt we were both there, that you were wanting it as much as I did. I thought, I honestly thought, we were making the journey together. But when the final moment came..." he paused, searching for the words "...suddenly I felt I was doing it alone. I'd lost you."

"Goddamn you, Jake Finlayson. We've both just had sex for the first time in a *year*—yes, me, too!—and now you want *pillow talk?* Just take the sex and *shut up.*"

He stretched out his hand to smooth away a strand of her hair that was lying across one of her breasts. His fingers were very gentle. "I didn't mean to make you mad, Miss Pain-in-the. I just care about you and want to know if I did anything wrong, so I can do better next time."

"Just because I wasn't screaming your name and going like 'Yes! Yes!' you assume I don't have orgasms?"

His smile was wry. "Something like that, yeah. But it was more than that. I felt I could almost pinpoint the moment you'd slipped off the wave."

She rolled her eyes. "I might have known a wave analogy was there, just waiting for me. Jeez. I'm really beginning to regret this. I'm fine, so why don't you head on back to the house and let me get some sleep."

That tone would have got any sane, *sensitive* guy out of her hair pretty damn quick, but not Jake Finlayson.

"Hmm." He regarded her for a minute. She was tempted to close her eyes to show him the conversation was terminated, but she didn't want him looking at her when she was, well, vulnerable. She chose instead to glare at him. But Jake was undeterred. "Have you ever had an orgasm?" he asked.

"None of your damned business!"

"Well, in this situation it sort of is." He still sounded apologetic, but with just the tiniest thread of laughter running underneath. Then his tone changed as he asked softly, "Do you ever wonder?"

She didn't need to ask what he meant. Her ability to stay calm in the toughest court, with the meanest judges and the most hostile witnesses, deserted her, and Sass felt her tears rise.

"Oh, shit, I'm sorry. I didn't mean to make you cry."

She dashed at her eyes with the back of her hand. "It's nothing. I'm just tired, so back off, okay?"

"Sure." He lay back down next to her. And sneaked a hand into hers. A friendly hand. She accepted it and they lay there on their backs, staring into the darkness. Sass felt stupid. No other lover—not that there were that many, considering she was over thirty years old—had ever picked up on her inability to orgasm, and it was something she'd learned to accept. She just wasn't the climaxing sort of girl.

Didn't mean she didn't enjoy sex. She did. It was simply that at the end of it, there was no rocket, no fireworks. She secretly wondered if all those movies and advertisements exaggerated the event. Sure, she'd read the magazines, got the odd book out of the library, but nothing helped. And that was okay, too, because in the end, she didn't need it. She enjoyed going to bed with men and knew enough to make them come back begging for more. That had been enough for her.

But now Jake had outed her. She'd never felt so

humiliated—even more so because of his gentleness. She could fight mockery, but was defenseless against his softer concern. So she decided it was time to out him, too.

"Why did you quit competitive surfing?"

He shifted uneasily and blew out a big breath. Ha. To his credit, he knew exactly what she was doing. "That's hardly fighting fair, Ms. Walker."

"I just *care* and want to *understand* you better."

She felt the bed vibrate with his laughter.

"You are such a bitch," he said amiably.

She smiled into the dark. "You haven't answered the question, Mr. Finlayson. But here's another. How did you get into it in the first place?"

"That's easy. I grew up surfing, but I'd never seen anything like those big waves until I went to Hawaii. It may sound crazy, but in a strange sort of way I felt as if I'd come home. Riding them is terrifying, of course, but man—the rush." He paused and she could feel him holding his breath, before exhaling long and slow. "There's nothing like it. Even sex," he added drily.

"So were you driven by some sort of death wish?"

He shook his head. "Not as such, no. It was more like a flirtation with the idea of death. There's this sick fascination and a belief that it's a price worth paying for the sheer exhilaration of one of those rides. Plus," he added, his tone shifting to self-mockery, "the adulation wasn't bad, either."

"Did all the girls fall in love with you?"

She felt the sharp splinter of something akin to jealousy—absurd, really. She never wanted commitment, so jealousy was never an issue.

"There were girls, yes. Also guys who wanted to be like us, and magazine shoots and sponsorships and wild parties. It was crazy. The only time anything felt real was waiting, scared shitless, for the next wave."

He fell silent and Sass waited. She always found it an effective way to get someone to talk.

"There was a girl on the circuit—Carole. Built like a goddess and a top surfer. Things got intense and she started wanting all the things I wasn't sure of, like marriage and kids, so I took off for a while, needing to get my head straight. I'd heard the waves were fantastic in Mozambique and I could have them all to myself, so I went there."

"You escaped to *Africa?*"

"Sure, why not? The waves are incredible."

It made sense, she supposed, remembering how the video had shown surfers flying around the world in search of the perfect wave.

His hand shifted in hers, his thumb tucking in to caress her palm. Sass had never felt anything so sensual in her life, but it was strangely relaxing, too. She felt herself splitting in two—with one part listening to a story that could only be confessed in the dark, the other vividly conscious of her desire for this man beside her.

"You've never seen such a beautiful coast. And yet the cities are still recovering from a vicious civil war—you see signs of it everywhere. I surfed a lot, slept a lot, lived very simply. Then one day, in the middle of nowhere, the ancient Jeep I was driving broke down. I began walking and that's when I came upon an orphanage. All these gorgeous little kids whose parents had died, mostly of AIDS. Many of them were suffering from AIDS themselves. They lived in primitive conditions, sleeping on mats, having lessons outside. The teacher was using this ancient piece of blackboard and the younger kids practiced their writing in the red dust. They only had one soggy old football. No computers, no TV, no mobiles—nothing. And yet I'd never seen anything like their joie de vivre." Sass could hear the smile in his voice as he said it.

"I stayed there a week and got to know Francesca, the Frenchwoman running the orphanage. Her strength and dedication are phenomenal. She's a couple of years older than me…and I was attracted to her."

Jake paused, and Sass thought again how she

had to be careful about inviting confidences. She really didn't want to hear about Francesca, who was probably a triple-orgasm-a-night woman. After all, she was French.

"She laughed at me and turned me down flat. It was a shock to the ego. She said I didn't know who I was and that I should try finding out sometime. That was insulting. I knew who I was. I was a contender for the world's Best Big Wave Rider.

"But that evening I sat looking out at the bush silhouetted against a red sunset, and began to wonder if anything I did was worth a damn. None of it made much sense in Africa. I left the next day. Saying goodbye to those kids ripped me apart."

"I hear you left them all your money."

The thumb stopped. "Who told you that?"

"Moana."

"That woman talks too much." But his thumb resumed its circular motion. Sass could feel him shrug. "The money's nothing. I was only wasting what I'd earned on what I'd thought of as the good life. It's doing one helluva lot more good over there. And Francesca is amazing—she gets every cent's worth out of a dollar. It's cool how the kids still write to me. If I ever get the money together, I'll go back one day."

He truly didn't give a damn that he'd given away a fortune.

"Didn't you agonize over it at all?" Sass had to ask. "I mean, you'd only known the kids for a week."

"What was there to agonize over? It was a no-brainer. New Porsche or decent facilities for the kids? Anyone would have come to the same decision."

She let that one pass. "So what happened?"

"I tracked Carole down. She was at the big competition being held at Mavericks in California. It has the wickedest waves in the world. I told her about the African experience and how I was ready for something more meaningful, and that I wouldn't be taking part in any more competitions. She asked me what I was going to do instead. I hadn't decided. Well, that ended that. She wanted to get married, yeah, but to a world-class surfer, not some loser with no life plan." He laughed. "She sounded just like my father when I told him I was going *into* surfing."

Jake unclasped his hand from Sass's and for a second she felt the hollowness of rejection. But he was only shifting position. He slid an arm under her neck, drawing her to him so that her head nestled into the muscles of his shoulder. With his arm around her, his thumb took up its rhythm once more, this time on the sensitive skin under her ear. It felt unbearably wonderful.

"Problem was," he continued lightly, "I truly didn't know what the hell I was going to do instead."

Sass was amazed. "Did you really stop big wave riding, just like that, after it'd been your life?"

"Well, I did go out one last time, the day after Carole and I broke up. It was a perfect dawn. The sky was clear and the waves were like glass. I had several stunning rides, then paddled out again, thinking, *this is it, this is the final one.* I waited and waited for the perfect wave. *Not this one,* I kept thinking, *the next might be better.* And then it struck me how dumb I was. Kids were starving, people were having bombs dropped on them and there I was, bobbing about on this God-given morning, worrying about which was the perfect wave. I caught the next one in."

Sass laughed. "And was it the best?"

"Course not. This is life, not the movies." He laughed, too. "It should have been the ride of my life, shouldn't it? The poetic end. It was good, great even, but nothing earthshattering. It didn't matter a damn. I flew home that afternoon."

They lay there in silence. What surprised Sass was how companionable it felt. In talking about Jake's life, her humiliation had dissipated. It was stupid to have got so riled up like that. After all, he'd climaxed. And he did make her feel great. All her bones had melted down to Jell-O. She was mesmerized by the thumb that still caressed her neck, but she was also aware of the firm skin beneath her cheek, the salty tang the man carried with him everywhere like cologne. Was this what pillow talk was all about, then? It was so *good.*

At the same time, her analytical mind was turning the evidence over. "I can't believe you threw everything away on a week's experience."

"Dreams change. The week was plenty long enough. I was seduced by the place, the kids, from Day One."

"But you didn't even return to them. You quit surfing and had nothing to take its place." She shook her head. "You're either really brave or ridiculously rash."

"Neither. At the risk of sounding hippy-dippy, I do believe that sometimes if you throw everything out, leave yourself open to fate, you're giving opportunities a chance. I enjoy my life now even though I'm crap at it."

Sass thought about the changes he'd made, the challenges he now faced.

"What sort of trouble had the boys been getting into before they came to you?"

"Usual guy stuff. Brad bounced from foster home to foster home and was picked up several times for hot-wiring cars and taking them on joyrides. Mike and Mark were chronic truants and shoplifting for kicks. Both divorced parents were into new relationships and not paying enough attention to them. They're with me until their mum and her new man find a bigger place. Their current house is too small, adding to their problems."

"What about Paul?"

Jake's arm tightened around her. "Your special boy. His family was a tight unit until his mum was killed in a hit-and-run accident. His dad couldn't cope, went into a severe depression and basically shut down. The poor kid became more and more introverted until one day at school he was found beating the shit out of one of the older boys. Broke the other guy's nose and several of his teeth before the teachers could haul Paul off."

"Paul?"

"Turned out the other boy had been laughing about how he'd hit a dog when he was speeding, describing how the animal had bounced over the bonnet and onto the roof. Much the same fate as Paul's mother." They were silent for a while before Jake continued, his voice grim. "I wanted to help the boys."

"You're doing a great job." Sass raised her head to look at him. "The kids are happy with you."

In the moonlight, she could see him smile.

"Happy, yes. Doing well, no. I'm not supervising them enough."

"All you need to do is set up some systems."

"I bet your whole life runs on systems."

"Hey, that sounds patronizing."

"Sorry. You're probably right, but you know, routines and lists are not my thing. What are *you* striving for?"

She was taken aback at the change of tone, the change of direction. "What?"

"I can't believe you don't have a life plan."

"Of course I do."

"And what is it?"

When she didn't say anything, he gave her shoulders a shake. "C'mon, tell me."

"There's a position coming up I'm hoping to get."

"What, in your company?"

"Yes."

Now it was his turn to be silent. Was it her imagination or did the darkness seem thicker, the air a fraction colder? She might have known he'd be onto it in a flash.

"So this resort is personally important to you?"

She had to be honest. "I didn't set the deal up, but now that it's in the pipeline, yes, it's in my interests, as well as in the company's, to see it through."

"This promotion, is it something you really want?"

"Want?" She gave a hollow laugh. "I've worked eighty-hour weeks these past seven years to prove I'm just as good as any male in our company. It's run by men who, though they'd never admit it, still have the deep-seated belief that a woman is too emotional to cut it at the top. Idiots like Kurt Branston can get away with schmoozing, but I have to prove myself or people will say I slept my way to the top. I want my achievements to be seen for what they are."

"So you hate this Kurt fellow as much as we do?"

"Probably more. You only had him for a few days. I've had him on my heels for five years."

In the ensuing silence, Sass discovered that she'd curled her fingers into Jake's chest as though she was clinging to him. She forced them to relax and lie flat.

The minutes ticked by and, despite the warmth of his body, she could feel herself going cold. She shouldn't have told him. She shouldn't have let him see. God, she was stupid to have let things get this far. Stupid, stupid, stupid. She had broken every one of her rules. Never show weakness. Never get rattled. Never get involved. What the hell had she been thinking? What the hell was Jake thinking now? She'd be damned, though, if she was going to ask.

Finally, he sighed.

"This has become very complicated."

Well, duh! She had warned him, hadn't she? And now he was going to pull away. Physical urges satiated, they could get back to business. She ought to pull away herself, but for some reason she just couldn't. She waited, a lump in her throat, for what he'd say next that would gently disentangle them.

"Tomorrow, Sass—that is today—I'd like to show you the terns. It's time you guys were introduced."

CHAPTER SEVENTEEN

SASS WOKE UP at daybreak when Jake kissed her on the forehead before sliding out of bed.

"Don't get up," he whispered. "I'm just heading back to the house before the boys know I'm gone. We're going out for a dawnie. Afterward I have to pop into town. You sleep in."

She smiled drowsily and murmured, "I'll be up soon. I never sleep in. Enjoy the surf."

The next time she woke up the sun was streaming into her room. She blinked, disorientated. When she glanced at her watch, she almost fell out of bed. Ten-thirty! What on earth was going on with her in this upside-down country? Jet lag, she thought. Plus two late nights and an early morning run. And dancing. She hadn't been dancing in months.

Then there had been the sex. It had been a long while since she'd last slept with someone, and her body still gently throbbed as though Jake had left his imprint on her, in her. Finally, there'd been all that talking—she who never talked. She was a listener, for chrissakes. It was ten-thirty and a night of follies lay behind her. But as her initial horror faded, it was replaced by a sense of languor. She stretched out, finding a cool spot in her rumpled sheets. There was still an indentation in the pillow next to her. Last night had been rash, last night had been mad and maddening—and incredible.

She lay there, replaying the fun with Moana, the dancing with Jake, the intimacy that came with sharing confidences in the dark. She veered away from focusing on the sex too much. It had, as she'd told Jake, been great. Enough said.

It was only when she heard his Jeep return that she finally scrambled out of bed and pulled on some clothes. Jake came up the steps. "Sass?"

"Yeah, I'm here."

She met him on her deck. He was looking his usual rumpled self, but he had something behind his back and a mischievous expression.

"Close your eyes and hold your hands out."

"What?"

"No, I'm not telling. Go on, close them."

After throwing him a look that told him she was not six years old, she closed her eyes and stretched out her hands.

"Whoa, what's this?" she said, as something very large and surprisingly light was placed across them.

"Wait!" Another light weight was added to the package in her hands. "Now you can look."

"A bodyboard?" She stared at it. "But I leave in a few days."

"Hell, you bought a coffee machine for a week, and this is way more fun than that!"

She shook her head and laughed. "Here, take it so I can open the box on top. What on earth is it? Not diamonds?"

"I can promise you faithfully it's not diamonds." Jake tucked the board under one brown arm, wearing a surf's-up, expectant grin as she unwrapped the box.

"Patches? Oh my God, you've got me nicotine patches!" Sass didn't know whether to laugh or be insulted. "But I don't want to quit smoking."

"You do, deep down," Jake assured her. "Just imagine conquering your only addiction. Once weaned off coffee and cigarettes, you'll be Ms. Invincible USA."

"Life won't be worth living. What possessed you? It's my business whether I smoke or not."

She plunked down on the step of the deck and stared at the packet. No one, *no one* had ever ambushed her like this before.

"I care," he said, leaning over to drop a light

kiss on the end of her nose. "Stop looking as if I've just handed you a nuclear bomb. It simply struck me as crazy to watch you tick the boys off about eating vegetables, and go jogging on that infernal machine every day, only to ruin it all with a few surreptitious fags snatched here and there."

"It's my business, not yours."

He sat down beside her. Today he was wearing cut-off denim shorts. She was not going to act sixteen and think how sexy he looked. "Of course it is, but seriously, Sass, you don't need that shit in your system. It'll lead to an early death."

He gave her a come-on-get-over-it nudge with his shoulder. She tried to suppress a smile. He gave her a bigger nudge.

"Hey, watch it. You nearly knocked me over."

"My intention exactly." Pushing her shoulders back, he bore her down onto the deck, where he proceeded to kiss her. It felt so good to have the sun hot on her face, the planks warm beneath her and his mouth covering hers. *If I could only freeze time,* she thought. Then they heard whooping and whistles and a couple of adolescents chanting, "Jake and Sass sitting in a tree, *K-I-S-S-I-N-G.*"

Jake groaned. "Bloody kids. I'd forgotten I told Brad I was popping over to get you to go surfing."

Sass and Jake struggled upright to see the boys

laughing as they scooped up their boards and disappeared up the driveway.

"Crap," she said, blushing. It was stupid, she knew, but she couldn't help feeling somehow busted.

"Don't rush on our account," Brad yelled.

"Cheeky buggers," Jake said, smiling.

"I thought you went surfing at dawn."

"We did. The waves are fantastic. That's why I bought you a board. You've got to come down and try them."

Sass demurred, feeling as if she was being swept out of her depth by Jake's enthusiasm.

"Kids do it," he insisted.

"I know, but I'd like to maintain some dignity."

"Who for? Me? The boys? There's only us out here. Come on, I'll be with you all the way."

"Don't you want to make the most of these fantastic waves?"

He shook his head. "No, you'll have my full attention. Today, Sass, you are going to ride the waves."

IT WAS FUN, she had to admit. Swimming out with the board was hard, especially when she was also learning to use the fins Jake provided, but bouncing over the waves took on a different dimension.

"Woo-hoo!" she cried as she ripped along the top of a wave and was carried up the beach. "I can see what you love about this sport."

Jake, who had body-surfed next to her, said simply, "No, that wasn't it."

"Whaddaya mean? That was great. Wonderful, in fact."

"You were just riding the white water."

"But it was fun."

"Sure, but it's not taking the drop."

She sat in the shallows, letting the spent waves lap around her. "Explain—in real English, if possible."

He settled next to her. "You stayed on the crest of the wave all the way in. Yes, it's fun—yes, you traveled. But taking the drop is when you actually go over the lip of the wave, just before it breaks. At that point it's pitched highest and smoothest, and you ride down the face of it, not on top."

"Let me get this straight. You catch it a split second before the wave breaks, is that right?"

"Yep." He swept his hair back with one hand, his eyes fixed on the sea. He could no more control his compunction to monitor the waves than she could control hers to smoke.

"So if your timing is off, you get bowled."

"Bowled?"

"Rolled over and over under the water."

"Right."

"Whereas if you stay on top of the wave, you always ride safely to the beach."

He turned back to her. "More or less," he said slowly. She knew he could see where this was heading.

"So why would I risk getting bowled, when I know I can have as good a time riding the white water?"

"Ah, but that's just it. Taking the drop is something else completely. Impossible to describe, but it has to be experienced at least once in your life."

"But I don't want to get bowled."

"You will, though—deal with it. I promise you it will all be worth it when you do take the drop." He saw her expression and added, "Trust me."

She snorted. "Yeah, right. Look where that got me last time! Soaking wet and shivering with cold."

"You loved it, you know you did. Come on."

So she got bowled and bowled again. Sometimes she rode the white wash and had fun. More often than not she was dragged up the beach in an undignified tangle of sand, board, limbs and hair.

"You aren't committing," Jake told her.

"I am so." Her throat burned with all the saltwater she'd swallowed. She kept lifting the leg of her swimsuit to empty out the sand.

"No, I've watched you. As soon as the wave lifts, at the very moment you should be paddling like mad, you ease off. You hesitate too long. Should I take this wave, yes, no, yes, no, and before you know it, it's come up and caught you."

So they went out again, Sass muttering imprecations against surf Nazis and wondering what the hell was so wrong with having a good time in the white wash, anyway. She was tired and fed up.

"I'm about done here," she called over to Jake. "The next wave will be my last one."

Jake barely acknowledged her. His whole attention was trained on the sea beyond. "This incoming set is looking great, Sass. You'd better get ready. All set? Go!"

She saw the swell moving toward her and began paddling.

"This one's it, Sass!" Jake's shouted. "Paddle harder."

Bastard, she thought. *Bully bastard, bully bastard.* The cussing gave her paddling rhythm and strength.

"That's right!" he yelled as she felt the wave pick her up. "This is it! Paddle and kick, kick, kick. *Commit.*"

She barely caught the last hurled word as suddenly she felt the wave's power simply take over. The board pitched and then she was over the lip, seeing the shimmering face below her. She fell with such speed, such power and such exhilaration that she couldn't keep from screaming out, "Yes!" as she swooped down the face, clinging to the board for dear life. It was almost like flying as she whooshed right up onto the shore, to grind to a halt in the sand.

Jake landed beside her, grinning. "Fun?" he inquired.

"Did you see me? I got it! I really caught it. I took the drop. It was incredible. That was the most amazing rush I've ever had." She was babbling but she didn't care. "I've just got to do it again."

He nodded. "Yeah. Now you know what I was talking about. So what are you doing lying here in the shallows when there are waves to be ridden?"

Much later she finally had to call it quits. Her arms ached. Her legs felt weak. Her body hurt in a dozen different places from where she'd been ground along the bottom, dropped on her head, bounced off her own board. She'd only succeeded in taking the drop another two times, but that didn't matter a damn. She felt great as she walked up the beach, bodyboard under her arm. No, not great, *sensational.* She leaned over to put the board down and scoop up her towel, then stood, drying her arms and toweling her hair as she looked out to the waves, where Jake and the boys were still playing. She, Sass Walker, had taken the drop. Her sense of achievement, of triumph, was absurd. Absurd and wonderful.

Jake rode in, bodysurfing the waves easily and joyously. Seal man. Merman. He paused in the shallows and she waved, then made shooing gestures with her hand to let him know she was fine by herself. He waved in acknowledgment, then turned, wading back thigh-deep before throwing himself full-length to swim out.

Sass spread out her towel and sank onto the sand. It was hot from a day's baking heat, and her muscles relaxed. This truly was paradise. A paradise families would flock to. She squinted against the glare of light bouncing off the waves, and tried to imagine this beach crowded with vacationers. Children building castles, teenagers playing volleyball and Frisbee, families under umbrellas, and well-oiled twentysomethings basting in the sun and sleeping off hangovers from the night before. In short, it would end up looking like the beaches of Spain, Greece, Hawaii, Brazil and all the other exquisite places around the world changed irrevocably by tourism. Something indeed would be lost.

Sass could understand Jake thinking it would be a travesty. But land deals were a fact of history. How, for example, had the Māori viewed the building of English houses on their ancestral lands? Manhattan Island had been sold for only sixty guilders. That was how the world developed. You might not like it but could you stop it?

She could.

She could save Aroha Bay, if nothing else. And lose everything she'd ever worked for. Lose the future she'd battled so hard to secure. For what? Jake had no money to buy the land himself to keep it safe, and besides, Sass was still not convinced of his long-term commitment to the bay and the birds. Certainly, they were the sole focus of his attention now, but he was a surfer. They were his ride at this moment in time. Soon something else would come along to catch his fancy, and in the meantime another developer would swoop down. In many ways the locals would be better with the devil they knew. Sass could at least ensure there'd be no high-rise hotels, no shopping malls, no casino. That was something.

She had to find a way to get Jake to see it was inevitable. She watched him swoop down another wave front, and felt a cold trickle of misgiving. He'd never accept it. He would hate her. She would wear the face of her company and he would despise her.

She could not bear even to imagine his loathing. And yet she simply could not surrender her career, her life, for a fling. Because it could never be anything more. What if she did throw the deal? Jake would get his bay, his birds and, social workers willing, his boys. For a while. Until his attention wandered. And what would she be left with?

A vision of her empty apartment flashed into her mind. She'd be left with nothing, zip.

There was no way she would stay with the company if Kurt got the promotion.

It was too ridiculous to contemplate. This was all her fault. She should never have broken her own damned rules. She should never have fallen victim to a pair of green eyes and an amazing body.

She deliberately kept her mind from suggesting her attraction to Jake was anything other than physical. She refused to think about the warmth of his writing, his charisma, his humor or his sensual, caring side. She blocked both the death-defying surfer and the exasperated, worried guardian. But even disregarding so many facets of his personality, she still found the scales tipped too far in his favor.

She had put herself into an appalling position, but since it was of her making, she must accept the consequences. A week ago she hadn't cared if Jake Finlayson hated her or not. So when his hatred did come—and it would—she would have to reach deep inside and locate that indifference that had become buried under a tumult of emotions and new experiences. It was going to be awful—the worst feeling no doubt of her life—but it was inevitable. In the end, nothing had changed except her feelings about Jake. All she could do now would be to enjoy it. Take the drop. Then quit the waves forever.

CHAPTER EIGHTEEN

AFTER LUNCH, Jake took her to see the terns.

"We'll be on sand so you won't need shoes," he said as he handed her binoculars, "but you might like these."

Sass kicked off her sandals and hung the binoculars around her neck. They banged against her chest as she walked.

"I can't believe I'm going *bird-watching,*" she remarked. "And you, buddy, look completely wrong for the game."

He glanced down at her. "How so?"

"You know, of the Lesser Spotted Nerd variety. No one would take you seriously as an ornithologist like this."

He was looking his usual gloriously rumpled self, eyes more vivid than ever, reflecting the green T-shirt he wore.

"You should be wearing a checked shirt and khaki shorts with lots of pockets filled with notebooks. Oh, and glasses, you should definitely be wearing glasses."

Jake tweaked her ponytail. "Talk about pots and kettles. What jury would ever take you seriously as some hotshot, up-herself lawyer?" He glanced appreciatively at her cropped T-shirt and short shorts.

"I'm not 'up myself,'" she said, backhanding him across his arm. "But I sure am one hotshot lawyer—and don't you forget it."

"I won't," he promised, and took her hand as if they were teenage kids on their first date.

It felt nice, walking hand in hand along the shore, the breeze ruffling their hair, the sand squeaking under their bare feet. The air in New Zealand smelled so *clean.* As she drew in a deep breath, Sass could feel her city lungs expand. Two seagulls wheeled above, and an oystercatcher prowled in the shallows, taking fussy-old-man steps. She loved the strength of Jake's hand with its callused palms. More DNA sequencing, she thought, from when women sought the best hunters to keep them alive.

They rounded the top end of Aroha Bay, scrambled around a small rise and then down onto the spit, where the sun was catching silver glints in the fine sand. Jake shortened his stride and his voice dropped to a murmur.

"We're coming into their territory. See that dune over there?" He pointed and Sass nodded.

"One family is usually there and another pair with one chick is farther along."

Suddenly there was a low cry as a bird swooped down, heading straight for them and pulling out of the dive only at the very last moment. "There she is," said Jake. "Mum coming in to protect her babies."

Sass looked up at the bird floating above them, still warning them off. It was slender, graceful, and seemed very small against the vast blue sweep of sky and sea. Only thirty-eight fairy terns left in the entire world. The full impact of the fact had been hard to absorb before. Now, seeing this mother hovering so protectively, and knowing how minimal their chances of survival were, Sass felt unexpectedly moved.

"Lie here." Jake pulled her down beside him so they were peering over the brow of a small dune. "The chicks will be somewhere out there."

The small clearing among the low dunes in front of them was littered with shell fragments and driftwood. A few balls of marine grass blew across the sand, reminding Sass of tumbleweed. A second bird materialized from over the ocean to also circle the area. The mother hovered in one spot, her earlier cries softened to chirrups.

"She's telling the chicks to stay still," Jake whispered. "They're almost impossible to see unless they move. Oh, look, she's coming in."

The bird's touchdown was light and she instantly froze. Sass blinked and for a second thought she'd lost the bird, the plumage blended so well with the surroundings. Lying on her stomach, propped up on her elbows, Sass lifted the binoculars and there, caught in the lenses, was an adult tern. The bird had a white belly and soft gray wings and back. The crown of its head was black, which, along with the elongated black eyes, gave the bird a dignified, almost aristocratic air. The legs and long narrow beak were orange. Extraordinary that such dramatic notes of color could disappear against the dunes, but they did.

"They're beautiful," she breathed, and Jake, only inches from her, turned his head and smiled.

"Aren't they?" he murmured. "The chicks are balls of gray fluff and they crouch low. Sometimes you can find them by their round eyes. Otherwise they look like part of the beach."

"Will they be near the mother?"

He shook his head. "The parents land away from the chicks to throw predators off the scent. They're canny wee birds."

His admiration was clear and Sass smiled to see this six-foot-three man entranced by a family of birds.

"Look, here comes the father."

The other parent landed in a different part of the beach and froze in turn, blending into the scene. Minutes passed. Sass watched the pair through the binoculars, marveling at them. Then she tried to find the chicks, sweeping the area systematically with her binoculars. Sometimes she paused at a curious twist of driftwood, or her attention would be caught by the glint of shiny fragments in the sand, but she couldn't find the chicks. Her eyes began to water with the effort.

"You try," she whispered, passing Jake the binoculars. While he was scanning the sand, she took the opportunity to look around her. The spit was narrow, with dunes running down its spine. Tufts of silver-khaki grass threaded them, binding them against the sea. The waves on the ocean side unraveled the length of the beach, leaving lacy patterns on the sand, while on the harbor side tiny waves washed the shore with a soft shushing sound.

A breeze tugged tendrils of hair out of her ponytail and they tickled her cheek. The sun was hot, the breaking waves as regular as a heartbeat. She was very aware of Jake's body lying beside her, could see sand caught in the fine hairs of his arms, which were braced, supporting the binoculars. His tangled curls created an almost halo effect under the sun. She had an urge to comb them with her fingers, bringing some order to their chaos. Not because she didn't like the chaos—far from it—but because it would take a while and there'd be no need for words or thought.

Sass blinked. This was ridiculous. They were supposed to be having a flirtation—time out from work and stress, time off from celibacy. Nothing more than that. Firmly, she resisted the impulse to lean toward him and inhale his own special scent of salt and soap and pure maleness.

"There," he breathed. "Gottcha, baby."

"Where?" He handed her the binoculars and put an arm around her back, to help point them in the right direction. The warm weight of it felt wonderful.

"Over there, do you see that piece of driftwood?"

"Yes."

"A baby's squatted in front of it. Can you see it?"

Sass stared till her eyes strained. "No." She was surprised at the depth of her disappointment.

The parents seemed to sense a baby had been spotted. *How could that be?* One flew up, wheeling, as fragile as a twist of paper in the sky, chirruping down. The other circled high, then came plummeting down at them time and time again.

"He's watched *Birds* one too many times," Jake murmured. Sass giggled, at the same time touched by the valiance of the tiny creatures.

"They sure are plucky."

Jake glanced sideways at her. "They are."

She could see he wanted to say something else. "What?"

He shook his head. "Nothing." But he removed his arm from her back. She knew he was thinking about the resort. She couldn't help thinking about it herself. There were only seven birds on this spit. Seven. Jake saw it as perfectly reasonable that they can a multimillion dollar project because of seven birds that might or might not make it anyway. She could feel the imprint of his arm on her back rapidly cool in the breeze. She wondered if he was going to push their case, but his attention had already gone back to the driftwood. He squinted against the sun, scanning thc nearby grass, then grunted in satisfaction and pointed toward the driftwood.

"There's the other."

Sass followed his finger and saw the grass ruffle as a tiny shape dashed from one end to the other.

"I saw it!" She was jubilant. "Sort of."

Jake laughed under his breath. "Good, they're both still alive, still safe. Now that we know where they are, we can get closer."

Silently, they rose and made their way down to the piece of driftwood.

"See it?" he asked.

Sass shook her head. "No." What was he talking about?

"Stop!"

There, in a hollow in front of her foot, was a tiny fluffball, speckled gray and white, exactly like the surrounding sand. Another step and she'd have crushed it.

"Oh!"

She finally understood. You could fence the birds off, sure, but if kids disobeyed signs and came racing in, the birds wouldn't stand a chance.

For a few minutes she and Jake stood looking down at the chick, which hadn't moved a feather. The tiny beak hadn't yet changed to orange and there was no hint of black on that tiny white, fuzzball head. Overhead the adult birds wheeled, screaming at them.

"We'd better go," Jake said. "We're stressing the parents. I'll check on the other family later."

As they walked back, they were silent and there was no lighthearted clasping of hands. Among the dunes, they'd drawn the battle lines, invisible but tangible.

Seven birds, that's all. But they symbolized the chasm separating them.

SASS HAD TO GET AWAY. She couldn't think in Aroha Bay. Jake's presence seemed to surround her, invade her, even now when he was out on the waves, coaching the boys again. Grabbing cigarettes and car key, she headed out. She knew she was driving too fast for the winding dirt road, but she didn't care. There was something burning inside her and she didn't like it. Wanted to outrun it. She lit a cigarette and drew in the first breath with something close to defiance. The tip glowed orange.

What was wrong with her? Usually she didn't agonize over things. Only this morning she'd resolved not to let sleeping with Jake influence her. After her bodysurfing, she'd been so sure the resort had to go ahead. But having seen the terns changed things, she couldn't deny it. It was one thing to hear about the possible extinction of a species, it was another to see some of the last surviving members.

Where was the middle road between the people of ABORD who just wanted jobs, and those few fragile birds?

Would Jake understand compromise? Of course he would. Then she pictured his stubborn mouth, his pugnacious jaw. No, he'd never forgive her. Next she thought of her company. *"We're counting on you, Sass."*

Pressing her foot harder on the accelerator, she veered around a corner. Things were just moving far too fast and were far too complicated. Her treacherous mind flipped back to Jake. To the dancing, to the sex. How he'd outed her. She groaned and took another pull on the cigarette. Then she thought about how he'd even accepted her lack of orgasm. He accepted so much—her background; her bossiness; even, it seemed, her inability to be a real woman. The only thing he found hard to accept was her job. Which was her. She was her job.

The thought crystallized as she ground out her cigarette in the ashtray with such force that it split open, spilling the last golden flakes of tobacco. She was here only because of the deal. That was her mission. People counted on her.

She eased her foot off the accelerator.

Jake Finlayson was a distraction—possibly even an infatuation—but nothing more. He, like the other men in her life, would disappear, and the gap left would spur her on to even greater success. It had been like that ever since her father had slammed out of their home for the final time, and she'd aced her exams the following week.

In the end she could only remain true to herself. The answer was out there. She just had to find it.

CHAPTER NINETEEN

THE DRIVE HELPED SASS restore her calm, and as she drove back down the driveway into Aroha Bay, she saw Jake was just putting his board away. The wind had come up in the afternoon and he was wearing a short black wetsuit that gleamed in the sun. He sauntered over to her car. His hair, as always, was awry, his eyes brilliant with adrenaline. He opened her car door and as she stepped out, he pulled her into a wet embrace, his lips salty on hers.

"Miss Pain-in-the, where've you been?"

"Ugh, you're soaking." Sass struggled, but it felt too good having those solid arms around her hot back, that laughing face so close to hers. Surrendering, she leaned in to deepen the kiss. Oh, Lordy, he was such a great kisser.

It was Jake who pulled back with a groan. "Man, a wetsuit is so not a thing to be wearing around a hot woman." They both looked down and laughed. "I've got to go have a shower—a cold one."

They linked hands as they began walking to the house. Jake fairly fizzed with energy, and the constraint that had lain between them at the spit had, for the moment, disappeared.

"Where did you go? You should have come out with us—though it was a bit big. You should have seen the waves. Brad got barreled several times. It was awesome. He's looking great for the comps. Paul's turns are really improving. And, oh, you should have seen the twins wipe out trying to learn to surf on one board."

Jake laughed and Sass joined him, loving this man who loved life.

"But what about you? Where did you go?"

They'd reached the steps of the deck and Jake dropped her hand so he could encircle her waist again. She leaned back against his arms, relishing their strength, and looked up into his face. "I went for a drive."

He grinned. "What? A drive? Just for the hell of it and time be damned? No way!"

"Yes way," she said primly. "I drove fast, too."

"I don't believe it. Miss Pain-in-the letting her hair down. That's so cool."

Leaning close, he kissed her again—a light, teasing kiss. When he pulled away, she made a small protest.

"No, you're just going to have to wait. I told you,

this is hardly the outfit to seduce a beautiful woman."

"True," she said, feigning disinterest. "Besides, you've had enough fun for one day, Jake Finlayson. You've got a book to finish."

"Madame Lash." He did a credible imitation of the sound of a whip cracking. "That's what I love about you."

He only said it as a joke, but Sass's heart gave a little jolt. What would it be like if he said the words when he wasn't teasing? Oh God, one night of sex and here she was, thoughts spiraling out of control as though she were fifteen again. *Brisk.* She must be brisk, and she broke out of the circle of his arms.

"We'll get onto it straight after dinner then," she said.

JAKE'S ENERGY AND HUMOR carried on through the meal. Was it the surfing or the sex? It galled her that she didn't know. That she cared.

Afterward, he brought out all his papers and dropped them with a bang onto the table next to her laptop.

"Right, I gave the book some thought out on the waves," Jake said. "If you can sort chapters four to eight, I'll rewrite the first three."

Sass nodded. "Okay, though you seem very

cheerful for someone throwing away hours and hours of work."

He handed her a wad of ill-sorted papers. "Actually, it really pisses me off, but bitching isn't going to get the job done."

"No," she said. "I guess it isn't."

She was surprised, however, at just how quickly he immersed himself in work. Surfing must have cleared his mind. After a faltering first few minutes, he began tapping away at a phenomenal speed. She tried not to think how endearing it was that he only used his two index fingers. He seemed as oblivious of her as of the shouts and laughter of the boys, playing Xbox in the next room. Once the guy locked onto something, his concentration was fierce—the concentration of a winner, a champion. No wonder Sass felt so good when all that attention was trained on her.

Her job tonight wasn't demanding, and in a strange way it helped settle her. She always took pleasure in bringing order out of chaos, and the formatting and renaming of files, plus watching the book take digital shape under her fingers, was calming. The whole time, however, she was aware that another part of her brain was busy processing all the arguments, sifting the information. She deliberately steered her thoughts away from it. Time to let the subconscious take over. The solution was close; she could feel it. But when it did come, she'd follow it through no matter how difficult. As Jake said, no point bitching.

Paul came in with cups of hot chocolate at ten o'clock, his middle ground between tea and coffee. The boys headed to bed soon after, and at midnight Jake's fingers slowed into a two-step staccato finish. He stretched back in his chair, rolled his head, then rubbed his face.

"Wow, what time is it? I'm exhausted."

Sass saved what she'd been working on and looked up. "I'm not surprised. You've been going at it for nearly three hours."

"So have you."

"Copying isn't the same as creating."

"Same punishment on the back," he said, getting out of his chair and wriggling his shoulders. "I'm not used to a desk job."

He came behind her and laid his hands either side of her neck. "How are you doing?" he asked, his massaging fingers exactly pinpointing tight areas in her muscles. With a groan of pleasure, she leaned back into his hands.

"How come you're so skilled at this?"

His thumbs circled out to release other areas of tension. "I learned from a masseuse."

"Don't tell me. A girlfriend?"

He remained silent.

"Well?"

"You said not to tell you."

She laughed. "Okay, wise guy. But I'm not jealous, just grateful. Too bad other girlfriends didn't teach you to cook or pay bills on time."

"Maybe that will be your legacy."

She laughed again, but this time she had to force it. One in a line of girls.

His lips touched the nape of her neck, trailed up to her ear. "Can I come with you to the sleep-out?"

Her heart stilled. "Sure."

Her excitement—and apprehension—welling, they made their way across the grass. She ached for him. No one had ever made her feel so good before. If he could only be satisfied with that. She was.

Inside the sleep-out, he pulled her to him. He caressed her neck, tracing her jawline with his thumbs. Then he fumbled at her bun.

"How the hell is this secured?"

She laughed, glad to break the almost unbearable sexual tension. "Ow, I'll do it."

"No, show me how. This is my fantasy and you'll spoil it if I can't do it myself."

She guided his fingers to the hairpins, and though he was still a little clumsy, he pulled them out one by one, and her hair fell to her shoulders.

"God, you are beautiful," he whispered, and kissed her, softly at first, then growing in intensity. Scooping her up in his arms, he carried her to the bed, where he very slowly undressed her, taking his time between each garment to thoroughly appreciate and arouse her body. Then he stripped in swift movements, his own body outlined in moonlight, behind him, the dark sea sequined with silver. Sass had never craved a man like this and reached out to pull him to her even as she knew she shouldn't—couldn't—let him get too close.

Although she'd never experienced an orgasm, she had had enough lovers to know how to set a man's passion ablaze. Their coupling was incredible. Even better than the night before. She moaned in her pleasure and rode on the crest of his ardor all the way up. Almost to the end. She put on a superb *When-Harry-Met-Sally* orgasmic display, though.

They both fell back, panting. She hoped this time he'd been fooled.

His hand found hers, his fingers tightening.

Don't say it, don't say it, she willed him.

"You are the sexiest woman I've ever been with."

Relief flooded her. She'd fooled him. He was no different from other men, after all.

"And the most complex."

Her fingers went limp in his as the air squeezed out her lungs. *Just leave it at that.* There were corners in her mind that even she never visited, and she sure as hell didn't want some guy blundering in.

Jake sighed deeply. "I hate that I can't satisfy you. Yet at the same time, I can't help feeling it's all tied up somehow."

She couldn't stop herself. "What?"

"Your immaculate appearance. Your efficiency. Your need to win. Your undentable niceness. Even your smoking."

Well, she had asked, but that did it. Tears welled up, yet she was damned if she was going to snuffle. Untangling her fingers from his, Sass rolled over, her back to him.

"It's late, so skip the psychoanalysis, okay?"

Jake didn't take the hint and leave, of course, but neither did he take offense. Instead, he curled around her, one hand cupping a breast as he kissed her hair.

"You are the most amazing lover. More than enough for me." Then, sounding frustrated and baffled, he added, "I just wish I could be enough for you."

You are. I'm just not woman enough for me.

CHAPTER TWENTY

THE FOLLOWING MORNING started off all wrong. Jake woke up feeling bad, to an empty bed.

For the second night he'd failed Sass, despite his very best efforts. He loathed failure, and to be failing in this particular department... He closed his eyes tightly for a minute. Had his year's celibacy lessened his performance? It wasn't him, it was her, hc assured himself. But even so... It just wasn't the sort of thing a guy would ever confess to—*I can't satisfy the woman I love.*

Like. The woman I like.

But it was stronger than that. He flipped over onto his back and studied the ceiling. He was, he decided, smitten. He liked the word. It conveyed a suitable amount of angst, but still had a temporary feel. He was smitten but he couldn't satisfy her. It not only made him question his own performance, it made him feel that, in some strange way, she held all the control, all the power.

If she cared about him the way he did about

her, wouldn't she have had an orgasm? Was it lack of trust? Lack of attraction? She was locked up and he didn't have a key. He stretched out a hand to the empty sheets beside him and had the strongest presentiment she was slipping away from him.

Jake got up, pulled on his shorts and walked out onto the deck, where he found her in the pale light of the dawn. She was sitting on the steps, laptop on knees, her fingers flying over the keyboard. She started when she heard his footstep behind her, and glanced up, her smile as bright as a shield. "Good morning."

It was like coming up against the Sass of one week ago. Bright, breezy—and beyond reach. She seemed to want to pretend nothing had happened last night—and face it, for her nothing *had.*

He dropped a kiss on the top of her head. "Good morning. What are you doing?"

It was an innocent question, but she'd tilted the lid slightly so he couldn't see the screen.

"An idea came to me in the night, that's all."

"Oh, yeah? What?" Her eyes were bright and there was a new resolve about her that he mistrusted.

"Nothing concrete yet. Going surfing?"

He knew then she was up to something for sure.

"Yeah, can you hear the waves? That's a good sign. I'll go wake the boys. See you for breakfast."

His smile was as fake as hers when he left. A surf was exactly what he needed to clear his thoughts.

THE WAVES, HOWEVER, did not cooperate. The conditions were lumpy, with lots of close-outs. Useful for learning in one way, as concentration was required to catch the right wave for a decent ride. Brad, though, wasn't trying at all. He kept taking any old wave, then trying to pull stupid stunts.

"Stop playing silly buggers and focus," Jake snapped.

Brad gave him the pitying look only a teenager can bestow on a slightly imbecilic adult. "What's your problem?"

Jake couldn't begin to explain what the real problem was.

"My problem is that the nationals are nearly here and you're just wasting your time and mine."

The kid shrugged. "Chill out, Jake."

That was all Jake needed. In crisp, no uncertain terms he ordered him off the waves and out of his sight.

Brad's expression tightened but he held on to his infuriating insouciance. "Sure, I'm happy to go. You need to lighten up, man."

"If you lighten up any more, a breeze will blow you away!" Jake yelled, but Brad had already gone.

BREAKFAST PASSED in silence, with Jake and Brad both still simmering. Sass and the twins initially attempted easy conversation but they soon gave up, and it was a relief all around when the boys took off to catch the school bus.

"What was all that about?" Sass asked as she cleaned her coffee machine. The faint scent of freshly ground coffee beans still lingered, and Jake realized how he'd come to like it. It was homey somehow. It didn't help his mood, however, as he put away the peanut butter and Vegemite and shut the pantry door with a vengeance.

"Brad's behaving like a brat. I don't get that kid at all."

Sass looked up at him for a second before saying, "He idolizes you. You do know that, don't you?"

Jake snorted. "Yeah, right. He doesn't take a thing seriously."

"You mean, he doesn't take surfing seriously."

"He's got talent like you wouldn't believe, but he's just pissing around, wasting it."

"Now you sound like your father."

Jake closed the fridge door with more unnecessary force. "I'm *nothing* like my dad."

Sass remained calm as she rinsed bowls under the tap. "You're exactly like him. That's why you fight so much."

But Jake was not in the mood to hear more. He escaped from the house to sort out the garage.

It was an hour later when Sass called, "Jake! Phone!"

He came inside and saw she was dressed up. Clearly, she was on her way to the city, and that just riled him more. What the hell was she up to? He snatched up the receiver. "Finlayson here."

"It's Miss Adderley, the principal's secretary." The woman's voice was glacial. "I'm phoning to tell you that Bradley hotwired the principal's car and was picked up by the police, traveling one hundred and sixty kilometers an hour outside town. Mr. King would appreciate it if you would come pick Bradley up."

Jake's hand fisted but he kept his voice level. "Thank you for letting me know. I'll be right there."

He slammed down the phone and found Sass at his elbow.

"What's up?"

He told her in a few terse sentences. She closed her eyes. "Oh, poor Brad."

"Poor Brad?" Jake was incredulous. "I'll have his guts for garters, so help me God."

He started toward the door, but Sass stayed him with a hand on his arm. "Jake, don't say anything you'll regret. He's just following in your footsteps."

For a second he didn't understand what she

meant. Then he got it. "Oh, no, no way! Don't even begin to compare my situation with his. It's not the same. I knew the risks when I took the dope to school. Brad's just a loose bloody cannon courting disaster."

Sass smiled. "I'd have loved to hear what your dad said the day your principal phoned."

Jake stormed out of the house without another word.

THE DRIVE IN GAVE JAKE the exact amount of time to recall every item on the long list of Brad's failings. He'd be expelled and then what? As for the way he was flushing his talent down the toilet... Words failed Jake. Added to which, he'd have a dickens of a fight with Janet to be able to keep Brad. He really didn't need this hassle right at this moment.

Jake marched into the school, where he found Brad sitting in the foyer, wearing the smoldering, defiant expression all teenagers seemed to have perfected. When he saw Jake, he raised his jaw as though inviting a punch.

"Come with me," Jake said curtly. "We'll deal with the principal together."

Then he could have bitten his tongue out. Those were the exact words his father *had* used. It was Sass's fault for having put the idea in his head in the first place.

The interview didn't take long. The principal reluctantly agreed not to press charges. He had intended to make an example of Brad, but when Jake pointed out that Brad could ill afford any more misdemeanors on his record, Mr. King finally conceded. He remained firm, however, on his decision to expel Brad. He was sure the school board would back him up. Jake was sure, too, and didn't try to fight it. Instead, like his father before him, he thanked the principal for having given Brad an education, and requested thanks be passed on to the teachers, too. Then, side by side, they walked out of the school forever.

"It's time you and I talked," Jake said.

They went down to a café at the marina, where Jake ordered two Cokes, even though he was dying for a beer. What should he say? He felt out of his depth and suddenly wished Sass was with him. She seemed to have a knack with the boys.

Brad swung back on his chair, his head tipped at a belligerent angle. In a hard voice he asked, "Do you want me to pack my bags today?"

Jake was taken aback. "What?"

"Do you want me out today or is tomorrow soon enough?"

"You're not going anywhere. I'm your guardian for the moment, whether you like it or not."

"You don't want me. Now you can get rid of me."

Jake stared. "Is *that* what this is all about?"

"No." But Brad wouldn't meet his eyes.

"Look, if you don't want to be with me anymore, you just have to say so. You're not a prisoner. You certainly didn't need to get expelled just to get away."

"It's you who doesn't want me."

"Oh, for God's sake! Just because I yelled at you?"

Brad stared at the ground, his mouth set in a mutinous line. Jake leaned forward over the table, resisting the impulse to grab the kid by the collar and shake some sense into him. "Listen, dumb-ass. Just because I yell at you doesn't mean I don't care. It means the opposite."

Brad remained silent.

"I know we have problems, but Finlaysons don't bail just because the going gets tough. And we sure as hell don't ever turn our backs on one another, no matter how pissed off we get."

"I'm not a Finlayson."

Jake sat back in his chair. "In my books, as good as. Let me make this clear. You can leave of your own accord, fine. But there'll always be a home for you at Aroha Bay."

Brad laughed bitterly. "Yeah, right. As though you'll be sticking around. You like to be free, hang loose. Life's just one big competition, and at the moment me and the guys and Aroha Bay are it. But once you've beaten the Americans, the tern chicks have flown and the nationals are over, what are you going to do?"

For a second Jake couldn't answer, unsure he still held the moral high ground. "This experiment was only ever short-term. They said they'd give it six months."

"And then what?" Brad glared at him. "We go back to our families and live happily ever after?" His tone was jeering but Jake could see the betrayal in the boy's eyes. He looked away.

Brad subsided back into his seat, his shoulders hunched forward as he noisily drained his glass through the straw, for all the world like an angry three-year-old. And, in some ways, as vulnerable. Brad hadn't seen his parents in years and his experience of foster homes was screw up and move on. The twins at least had each other, and the frequent phone calls and regular weekend visits suggested that, when the time came, they'd be happy to go back to one parent or another. What about Paul? Jake had just assumed his dad would be well in a few months. But what if he wasn't? Would Paul have to look after *him?* It would be far too big a responsibility for a fourteen-year-old.

Dammit, Brad was right. When he'd taken the boys on, Jake had thought it would be fun—guys hanging out together, the boys learning from him like some sort of goddamn guru. He hadn't thought it would ever get to this stage. One thing was clear, though. He was the adult, he'd better start playing the role.

"Well," he said to break the silence, "how about you tell me what happened."

"You know what happened."

"Yeah, well, tell me from your perspective."

He thought Brad wasn't going to say anything as he sat fiddling with the straw, so he waited. Sass liked to use this "silence" technique. Eventually Brad shrugged.

"It was nothing. I was bored. The car was there." Then he looked up, his expression hard. "I'm not sorry."

Jake rubbed his jaw with the back of his hand. "I didn't think you were. It doesn't matter, you know, about school. You can still be a top surfer—you've just got to commit. That's why I get so frustrated with you. You've got to hunger for success to achieve it."

Brad's voice was very low as he said, "What if I don't want it?"

"You don't want to be champion surfer?" Jake couldn't believe it.

"Why do I have to live your dream?"

There was a stunned silence, then Jake gave

a shout of laughter. Brad's expression turned to one of bewilderment.

"What are you laughing at?"

This just made Jake laugh harder. It must have been the release from the day's tension, but once he started, he couldn't stop. After a minute Brad grinned uncertainly.

"I don't get it."

"You've turned me into my father, you little bastard."

That made Brad laugh, too, and the strain between them evaporated. When Jake at last regained his composure, he leaned forward and clinked glasses. "Welcome to the world of expulsion, and tell me what it is you really want to do."

"I want to be a mechanic. Yeah, I know you can't believe it, but some of us like engines—love engines." He paused and looked out over the boats. Jake could see him debating whether to say something more.

"Okay. What else?"

"It would be cool to work on racing cars," Brad mumbled. "Maybe become a racer myself."

"I should have guessed." Jake thought for a minute. "A friend of my dad owns a racing car. Would you like me to talk to him and see where we go from here?"

Hope lit Brad's face. "You'd do that?" Then he

looked suspicious. "Your old man won't want to help a kid like me."

"Like me, you mean," Jake said. "Sure he would. He'll moan and lecture and say I'm a crap guardian and that you've squandered the best opportunity you'll ever have in your life, and then he'll phone his mate. That's just how he is."

As he said that, Jake felt an unexpected surge of pride in his father. That really was how the crusty old guy did things. Now, watching Brad turn his back on a promising career, he finally understood how much he'd hurt his dad. And while Matt couldn't resist sniping and interfering, he'd always had his sons' backs. He'd given Jake the money to fly to Hawaii for his first international surfing comps.

Jake shoved his chair back and stood. "Come on, then, we'd better get going so that we can make those phone calls."

"Really?"

Jake cuffed Brad across his ear. "Really, you dumb-ass. And know this, no matter where in the world I am, there'll always be a floor you can sleep on. Got it?"

"Got it." And Brad's smile made Jake think having kids might be okay, after all.

CHAPTER TWENTY-ONE

WHEN SASS GOT HOME she looked tired, but there was a quiet resolve about her that made Jake wonder what she'd been doing all day. There was no chance to ask, however, as a jubilant Brad buttonholed her immediately.

"I've got a job! One of the mechanics in Whangarimu has agreed to let me work with him, and on weekends I can travel down to Auckland to hang out at the racetrack and help out a friend of Jake's old man."

"Really? That's just great, Brad." She looked genuinely pleased even though she, like Jake's father, would no doubt have preferred he remain in school. After she'd changed, she returned to the kitchen to begin cooking, and Jake went to help her.

"What are you making?"

"Fajitas. Wow, Brad's like a kid with the best Santa present ever. You're looking pretty damned happy, too."

Jake got a bottle of pinot gris out of the fridge

and poured them both a glass. His early morning temper seemed a long time ago. Now he was just very happy to see her and wanted to talk about the day with her.

"I still don't get how he can just turn his back on surfing but he says he only wants to do it for fun. Go figure."

Jake handed Sass a glass and she took a sip. There was mischief in her eyes as she asked, "So was it hard for you Kiwi males to talk?"

He leaned back against the kitchen bench and thought how good this felt, chatting about the kids over making dinner. "Not as hard as I thought it might be. Once I started sounding like my father, I quite got into the swing of things."

Sass picked up a knife and began chopping. "You sounded like your father?"

"Don't laugh at me like that. It was the most horrible experience. I think I was even quoting him word for word at one stage. Worst of all, I began to understand him."

"Jake Finlayson, I do declare you may be beginning to grow up, after all." She turned and waited, eyebrow arched. "Go on, admit it now."

He pretended ignorance, then relented. "Yes, you're right. I'm like my old man for better or worse—worse, I suspect."

She laughed and turned back to her chopping.

"Come off it, Matt's fine. He's got charm and he's very successful."

"Yeah, but more than that, he's loyal."

There must have been something in his voice because she paused. "I realized today," Jake went on, "that even though he must have been gutted when I rejected all he stood for, still he came up with the money to send me off on my 'crazy schemes' as he put it. I owe him. Not for the money. I repaid that as soon as I could. But I owe him in that I never once thought he'd ever throw me out. That's what Brad was expecting. He thought I was going to make him pack his bags tonight."

"Poor kid."

"I explained that Finlaysons don't do that. We stay together through thick and thin."

Her chopping faltered, just for a second, and Jake could have kicked himself. How could he have forgotten her family seemed estranged from each other?

"So a mechanic, hey," he said to cover the awkward moment as he got lettuce and tomatoes out of the fridge.

"Yeah, cool." Sass's voice was flat.

Better to attempt a change of subject altogether. "How was your work today?"

"Interesting."

He wasn't going to let her block him. He'd

managed to talk things out with Brad; he could do it with Sass, too. Switching on the tap to rinse the leaves, he said, "Do you know that's what you say when you're ducking a subject?"

"No, do I?"

Jake crossed to her. "And now you're going into your untouchable mode. That's what you do when you don't want me to know how you're feeling. That's what you were like when you came home. How you were this morning."

"Really?" She flicked him a glance, her eyes guarded.

"Really." He knew not to move into her space, so began chopping tomatoes on the other counter as she turned on the stove. "C'mon, Sass, don't shut me out. Tell me what you're thinking."

"I'm thinking about dinner."

He was determined not to let her duck out this time. "Sorry I hit a nerve talking about my family like that. I didn't mean to."

"No problem, my family is my own business."

She turned the heat up so the oil began to hiss. Still Jake persisted. He'd been serious when he'd said it was all related. The key to her letting go had to lie here.

"So how did you guys fall apart?"

She was silent so long he thought she wasn't going to answer. He could smell the spices she flung into the pan, and the chicken that followed shortly after. When she finally began speaking, Jake had to stop chopping so he could hear, her voice was so low.

"The last time we were together was Cole's trial, the day he was sentenced. Mom was juiced, of course, and Adam was full of talk about busting his brother out—it was before he had the crap knocked out of him in his motorbike accident. None of us could get through to each other at all. Then I made Cole angry when I went to visit him by saying that this could be a great opportunity to finish his education. There he was, hating himself, hating the world, and he landed up hating me, too.

"Last time I visited, Mom had been drinking and just kept quoting poetry. I decided I didn't need all this in my life. And Adam, he went away on his bike and never contacted me, not even when he had his accident. So there you are. The Finlaysons we are not."

Jake crossed to where she was standing, her back to him and put his arms around her, pulling her against his chest. He didn't know what to say. She stayed rigid. He kissed one of her ears.

"I told Brad that as far as we're concerned, he's a Finlayson now. There's no way any of my family would ever turn him away. The same goes for you, too. You're part of the whanau now, whether you like it or not."

She turned in his arms and looked up into his face, troubled, and he wondered again what her work had been about today. She looked as if she was about to say something when Mike and Mark burst into the kitchen. They stopped short in the doorway and made retching noises.

"No wonder dinner's late!" Mike said.

"Get a room—but finish cooking first."

Sass laughed and broke out of Jake's hold. "Go set the table," she said. "Dinner's in five."

Jake returned to his salad. Must be all the court training, he thought, that made her able to mask her true feelings so swiftly.

AFTER DINNER, Jake settled down to his book. Sass had finished off what she could do to help him, and was now playing cards with the boys. There was a burst of laughter from the lounge and he glanced up. Through the half-open door, he could see them sitting cross-legged around the coffee table, playing five hundred. Sass was facing his direction, completely absorbed as she dealt the cards, then sorted her hand with deft decisiveness. Her expression gave nothing away.

The new game began and Jake pushed back his chair to get a better view. Sass gave no quarter as she quietly but efficiently scooped up the tricks.

"Oh, what? Have you won again?" Brad said in disgust. "We've got to step it up or she'll annihilate us."

Paul was bewildered. "But I had a good hand."

Sass smiled, sympathetic yet brisk. "You played too rashly. I knew your hand after the first trick. Sorry."

Paul shook his head. "How did you get to be so good?"

"By losing lots. That's how life works. Your turn to shuffle, Mark." She shoved the cards across to him.

Jake missed what Mark said, but everyone laughed. He watched Sass bring her chin up as she threw the miscreant a mock-warning glance.

"You watch your back, boy." It was a great cowboy drawl. Her fair hair was pulled into a pony tail. The night was hot and she was wearing a tank top and shorts. She could have passed for sixteen. He thought about the black trousers she wore for business, the outrageous leggings for the *Grease* party. There was also the woman who, just over a week ago, had arrived in heels and a suit designed to intimidate. Then he thought of her lying stretched out and naked, impossibly beautiful.

Could she really be that many different types

of woman or were some facades? If so, which were facades? He watched as she deadpanned her way to another win. She played her cards close to her chest and she played to win. He'd let himself forget far too much these past few days. He'd taken his eye momentarily off the ball, but today with Brad he'd realized how important it was to honor commitments and see them through to the end. Sass was right to be putting space between them. Sleeping with the enemy had proved to be a really dumb idea.

CHAPTER TWENTY-TWO

THAT NIGHT, they didn't sleep together. As she left the house, Sass murmured something about being very tired, and Jake felt in no mood to follow. The feeling that she was up to something was stronger than ever, leaving him powerless and angry. His suspicions were confirmed the following morning when she announced she was going away for a few days, as there were things she wanted to check out. With her customary efficiency, she was gone within half an hour.

The house seemed quieter without her. Which was stupid to say with four rambunctious teenagers about the place, but Jake could tell they missed her. Though they were vociferous in deriding his cooking, there was something generally lacking in the conversations over dinner. Sass had a way of drawing them out, finding out how their days had gone. Without her, they simply fell back into old patterns of good-natured abuse. When Jake tried asking them about school and work, he received either monosyllabic or mocking replies to his questions.

Then there was the disappearance of what Jake could only identify vaguely as the feminine touch. He insisted the boys keep to the routines she'd set up, but she had a way of doing small things like plumping cushions and filling jars with flowers that turned the house into a home. He even missed the smell of freshly ground coffee.

As for himself, Jake found he missed the companionship of their late-night hot drinks together. He missed her wit, their shared concern for the boys. He missed the sex—God, he missed the sex. But he missed small things, too, like the way she tucked her hair behind her ears as she got down to work. Her slow, Southern voice. Her twilight eyes.

The weekdays limped along slowly and on Friday Jake awoke at dawn after another crap night of broken sleep. What was the big deal, anyway? he wondered as he flipped onto his back. He'd got what he'd wanted—a few nights of, for him, great sex with a beautiful woman. So what if it was over?

Except that it clearly wasn't. As the night began to lighten, he finally faced the unpalatable truth. Somehow, during the past couple of weeks, she'd sneaked in and planted her Texas flag in his heart. And he didn't know what the hell to do about that.

Unable to lie still, Jake pulled on surf shorts and prowled into the kitchen. He glanced out the window and did a double take. Parked next to his Jeep was a jaunty red convertible. Light spilled down the steps of the sleep-out.

The grass was wet with dew as he padded over in bare feet, thoughts and emotions turbulent in contrast to the harbor waters, which were flat and tinged pink under a blueing sky. It was going to be another hot day.

"Sass?" he called softly as he came up the steps to the sliding doors, which were open. The sight inside stopped him dead. Sass, hair pulled back in a ponytail, was standing over the last of some pages coming out of her travel printer.

"Where have you been? What time did you come home? Why didn't you wake me?"

She spun around, and for the briefest second he thought he saw something like joy flash across her face. But it was immediately replaced by her smile—her professional smile.

"Hey, Jake. I've been down in Auckland, checking out an idea of mine, chatting to experts. I came home at 2:00 a.m. and I didn't want to disturb you guys."

You guys. She was lumping him in with the boys.

He'd been turning himself inside out all week and she'd been off doing her thing, clearly not sparing one thought for him. The idea burned. Then he saw a fat pile of papers sitting on the table. The front page in bold, black type read "The Aroha Bay Resort." The hairs on his arms rose.

"What's this?"

"It's a draft of the report. I've just finished it." She straightened, her hand going protectively to the pile. There were smudges of fatigue under her eyes.

He could feel his lip curl into an ugly smile. "I see that. So you've made your decision."

"Yes."

Her voice was steady, but she gave a little half shrug that might have been apologetic, might have been dismissive.

It didn't feel real—but at the same time it felt all too horribly real. He stepped into the sleep-out, narrowing the distance between them. "You're going to recommend the resort go ahead, aren't you?"

She couldn't quite meet his eyes. "You know my report is confidential. I've made that clear from the start. But, Jake, once you read it I think you'll find—"

He raised his hand to stop her. "Don't explain. Don't justify. It's a resort. Enough said."

Anger and a new sort of pain he'd never experienced curdled his stomach. She'd warned him that he'd mix their relationship with resort issues, but he hadn't listened, stupidly confident he could stay detached—the way she clearly had. He was such a fool. He closed his eyes, suddenly cold with the knowledge that Sass was about to destroy his world and there was nothing on earth he could do to stop her.

But, by God, he would try.

SASS ONLY GLIMPSED his hurt and betrayal before his eyes opened, burning with fury. His jaw—that lovely, pugnacious jaw she'd feathered with kisses—hardened as he squared his body for war. She'd known this moment would come, but still felt nauseous. All week she'd been functioning well on an intellectual plane, taking joy in seeing the way forward. Away from Jake, it was all so obvious. But in unguarded moments and alone at night she'd been unable to avoid despair. An uncompromising opponent, he'd never forgive her.

When he'd arrived on her doorstep, wearing only surf shorts, with his hair sleep-rumpled, her heart had bucked. In another universe she would have leaped at him, wrapping her legs around his waist, her arms around his neck, relishing the power of the man as he held her close to his solid chest. But she'd chosen a different universe this week. That could never happen now. The only way through was to keep everything calm, everything rational. Emotions had no place here—not anymore. Still, she had to try once more to reassure and convince him.

"Jake, it's not what you think it is. I've listened to you, read your book, seen the terns. Believe me, I understand how you feel, and it hasn't been easy, balancing that against ABORD. I've given everything I've heard due consideration..." She faltered, seeing his expression.

"Really?" His voice was heavy with sarcasm. "When exactly did this consideration take place? When we were out surfing? Bird watching?" He seared her with a look. "Making love?"

"That's unfair, Jake." Her voice was calm even as her hands shook. "I gave everyone a fair hearing and then on Sunday night I saw a solution. I've been meeting with other parties down in Auckland, checking out if my idea could work. And it can, it really can if you give it a chance."

"You listened but it's no coincidence that your recommendations should so neatly serve your company's best interests," he said. "All the time you smiled and seemed so nice." He laughed. "You even got to enjoy the entertainments laid on by the locals."

She could still turn this around. She could. She was the queen of negotiation. Honesty was always her strongest weapon. "Jake, I wasn't playing. What we had was—"

"Don't say real!"

She put a hand on his arm. "Special. Unexpected. God knows I was never looking for it. Didn't want it, even."

"Thanks."

"But I couldn't resist."

He stared down at her, eyes as cold as glass, and shook off her hand. "Neither could I, but I wish I had. I can't believe that after everything, we're still going to get some bloody Jungle Paradise and to *hell* with everyone down here. You, Sass Walker, are going to betray us all."

And just like that, her temper flared. Jake had succeeded in goading her as no New York lawyer ever had.

"Don't you dare talk to me about disregarding other people," she said, vibrating with anger. "I've done nothing but listen all week, which is more than you have ever done, Jake."

"What do you mean?"

"Just that." She took a step closer. "Have you ever listened to ABORD, really listened? They're nice people who just want jobs, opportunities. Not everyone is born with a whopping great silver spoon in their mouth and the talent to do anything they choose."

He folded his arms across his bare chest and stared down his nose at her. "The local economy is hardly my fault."

"No, but you could play a part in trying to improve it. Money may not be a big deal to you, but it's huge to most people. Don't you see that it's only because, deep down, you know you'll always be rich that you can give away fortunes? Look where you live. Most people don't have this luxury. *Or* the luxury to give away their money."

He flinched but said through gritted teeth, "Don't throw my family's wealth in my face just because you have some trailer park complex."

His words lashed her. "You bastard! You are so blindly selfish it's amazing you've managed to find your way around the world at all. I mean, just look at Aroha Bay."

"What the hell are you talking about?"

She gestured to the peaceful dawn tide behind him. "You want to keep it unspoiled, right? But I don't see you moving yourself and the boys back into town, tearing down this house and letting it all go back to nature. What you mean is you want to keep it as it is where only you guys get to enjoy paradise. Well, I've got news for you, buddy, *everyone* is entitled to a week in paradise.

Everyone. That's what holidays are all about. For a short time, people get the chance to live the dream you wallow in day after day."

Her words hit him like bullets. He recoiled but was plainly furious now. "What about the terns?"

"I know." She felt anguish, but was on the road of no return now. "But, Jake, we are talking about seven birds. Seven! You yourself cannot guarantee they'll be around in a few years' time. All we can do is try to protect them."

"Yeah, right, by building a resort." He seized her by both arms. "You are going to go ahead, aren't you, despite the birds—despite the boys. Despite me, for God's sake—despite us."

For a second she felt ripped apart. His grip was tight but she knew he must be exerting monumental self-control not to crush her.

She looked into his face, white with fury, and knew with cold certainty that if there ever had been an "us", there wasn't any longer. Texan through and through, she went in, guns blazing.

"Don't you dare try playing that card. What we had was never about this."

His fingers tightened and he pulled her closer. "It was all about this."

"Not for me."

His bare chest was only centimeters away, but she tipped her head to eyeball him.

"What's really going on here, Jake," she added, "is that you can suddenly see you might lose."

His eyes blazed as he abruptly released her and took a step back. She could tell he was only just holding violent emotions in check, but couldn't stop herself from going in for the kill.

"Yes, you, Mr. Champion. You can't bear the thought of not getting your way. Are you really fighting my company or are you fighting your father? You know all your privileges have come from deals exactly like this one, and you hate that. Most of all, you hate that when you look at your father, you see yourself staring right back."

"What about you? You spend all your time on crap like this—" he snatched her report off the table and waved it in the air "—because you are too bloody scared to take a real look at your life. You think if you pin everything down into lists and routines and reports, you can make yourself invulnerable. Don't open yourself up, and life doesn't get messy. Well, news flash. Life's all about messy!"

He threw the report at the wall and it exploded, white pages flying in all directions. She cried out, but Jake wasn't finished, and he rounded on her again.

"You say I'm like my old man. Well, let me tell you, Sass, that *you* are your father's daughter."

His words hit like a blow to the face.

"That's crazy, you've never met him. Hell, I haven't seen him since I was twelve years old. How can you say—even think—something that idiotic?"

"Think about it. He's not the only one who walked out on your family. You criticize me for only taking on short-term commitments, but at least they *are* commitments. You've locked yourself away so there's no room for any commitments at all—apart, of course, from your company. The company you've been trying to be the perfect daughter to all these years, only they've never noticed."

"How dare you!" She bunched her fists at her sides, but he wasn't finished yet.

"The only outlet you allow yourself at all in your uptight, battened-down world is your damned smoking. I bet you took it up as the one defiant action in your whole conforming life, and here you are, twenty years later, still acting out like a teenager."

"Shut up. Shut up!"

"You ran out on your family when things got tough and now you're running out on me." He stopped short as enlightenment dawned. "Oh my God, that's it, isn't it? That's what this rush is all about. We got close, *I* got too close—and now you're running, using work, as always, as your goddamn excuse."

His words stripped her down to bare fury such as she'd never experienced since the day her father had left. There was no one she had to protect anymore; no little brothers to have to pretend to that everything was okay and not some nightmare that would never be right. She could yell at Jake like she could never attack her mother. She wouldn't lose her job over this….

Red-hot anger erupted after decades of repression, and she launched herself at him, fists pounding, nails scratching, feet kicking as she hurled cuss words she'd never realized she even knew.

He grabbed her by both arms, pinning them to her sides, and pulled her to his chest, kissing her. She bit his lip, tasted blood with almost savage pleasure. She raked his bared chest with her fingernails. He tore off her blouse and bra as, locked in combat, they fell onto the bed. His shorts, her skirt fell away as over and over they rolled, punishing each other. Claiming each other.

Sass's anger was mixed with desperation, sorrow and pure, mindless passion. As Jake pushed into her, she was beyond any rational thinking, and when he began his pounding rhythm she rose to it, spurring him faster and more furiously, as though to burn every last conscious thought from her mind. She locked eyes with him, hating him for having made her love him, loving him for unleashing all her rage, her pain. He was never going to speak to her again, but he'd remember her. Then she was caught up, swept away in pounding waves of pleasure she'd never experienced before.

"Say it," Jake gasped, eyes blazing into hers, "damn you, say it."

And so she finally came in a tumultuous surge, crying his name out, over and over.

CHAPTER TWENTY-THREE

JAKE LEFT IMMEDIATELY after tugging on his shorts. He didn't look at her. Didn't say a word.

Shaken, Sass crawled off the bed. Slowly, she began picking up the pages one by one, clutching them in a fist against her bare breasts. She would have to print out other copies. And she would. What had just happened didn't alter her opinion. In the end, she wouldn't allow the other considerations to interfere with business.

She lay the crumpled sheets on the desk, flattening them out with one shaking hand, then headed for the shower.

As the hot water poured over her head, she finally abandoned herself to her grief. She couldn't remember the last time she'd cried other than at the movies. It was with relief that she let tears roll down her face. They mingled with the scalding water and were erased. After a while, she reined herself in and began scrubbing. She rubbed her scalp, then her arms, her legs, her stomach, her butt and her breasts until she was tingling and raw. But nothing could distract her from the treacherous warmth that still infused her. Jake, damn him, had woken that part of her she'd never believed existed, and then he'd gone, just like that. She heard again and again in her head the slam of the screen door as her father had abandoned them, leaving her mother a sobbing wreck for his daughter to pick up.

The water was running cold by the time Sass stepped out of the shower. She dressed very slowly, with care, in her white skirt and turquoise blouse. The collar would hide the two bites already emerging on her neck. She scraped her hair back into a bun. Her eyes in the tiny mirror were red, and she applied eyedrops, then mascara. Her mouth was swollen so she didn't bother with lip gloss. What did Jake's back look like? she wondered. His neck? Where had that bloodlusting harpy come from? Outside her window she heard the tumbling song of some bird as it perched on the flax bushes.

Then she heard running outside the shed.

"Sass!" Mike yelled. "Phone for you. It's America."

Her heart lurched. Surely, surely, it wasn't Kurt phoning to gloat.

"I'm coming now. Tell them to wait."

Sass ran across the lawn in bare feet and dashed into the TV room, where Mike handed her the phone.

"Hello, Sass here."

"Sass?"

Her knees sagged when she heard the warm Texan twang. Of all the people she wasn't expecting.

"Adam? Is that really you?"

"I'm so glad to finally get you. I've been trying for hours. Is your phone dead?"

"I'm out of cell range."

"In the end your office put me in touch with this guy, Rob Finlayson, and he gave me this number. It's about Mom. She's been hospitalized. They say it's bad." His voice cracked. "She may die."

Sass swayed and suddenly, miraculously, there was a hand under her elbow, supporting her to a chair. Jake. He had pulled on a T-shirt, all trace of anger gone. There was only concern in his expression now.

"What is it?" she said into the phone.

"Pneumonia. She's really let herself go this past year."

"Why didn't you get in touch with me sooner?" Sass sounded shrill even to her own ears.

"You know Mom. She has her pride."

Yes, Sass knew. That's why they'd lived in a trailer park rather than go back to her grandparents.

"She couldn't bear for you to see what she was turning into."

Sass closed her eyes and leaned back in the chair. Jake placed a hand on her shoulder and she rubbed her cheek against it.

"She's asking for you," Adam said. "Can you come?"

"Of course. First flight I can catch. Tell her that. Tell her to hang on. Can you do that?"

"Of course I can." She could hear the note of indignation. "I'm not entirely useless."

"I didn't mean it that way." Her fault. All those years of nagging at him, niggling away. "I'm sorry it came out that way. You've done great. You're there for Mom and you've found me at the bottom of the world."

He laughed. "You'll have to tell me what the hell you're doing down there, but I gotta go now. The doctor's waiting to talk to me. You've got my number, right? Phone me with flight details and I'll pick you up."

Tears blurred her vision. "On your motorbike?"

"Nah, I remember how you travel. I'll borrow a car for all your suitcases. See ya soon."

Sass lowered the phone. Jake just stood, hand

on her shoulder. With an effort, she rose and his hand fell away.

"My mom's ill. I've got to get home."

He nodded. "Where are you flying to? I'll get you a flight while you pack."

She liked that he didn't sympathize. That would have started her crying. "Houston. Money's no problem. I'll pay anything, okay?"

He nodded again and gave her a gentle shove toward the door. "Go. I've got this end covered."

BECAUSE IT WAS HARD TO see through the sheen of tears, Sass didn't pack with her usual care. She half-folded some garments, crammed others. She even sat on one suitcase to make it close. Finally everything was somehow shoved away and her bags stood in a line. The sleep-out was strangely impersonal again, after being home for a fortnight. Only the rumpled bed indicated habitation. There was a footstep outside and Jake appeared in the doorway, silhouetted against the sunlight.

"I've got you the flights. We've an hour before we need to leave for the airport. You'll fly to Auckland and from there straight on to L.A., where you pick up the next connection."

She nodded, unable to look at him. "Thanks."

"Sass?" She kept her head down. He stepped closer, then hesitated. "I'm so sorry. I've never lost it like that in my life. I was way out of line. I'm appalled at myself. Did I—I hope I didn't hurt you?"

She shook her head. "No, you didn't hurt me." She burst into tears. He pulled her into his arms and she sobbed into his chest, feeling as if she was in both a dream and a nightmare.

Jake stroked her back, dropping kisses on the top of her head. Then his arms tightened as though he didn't want to let her go.

"I want to sleep with you," she whispered. "Just one more time."

He loosened his hold so he could lean back and look into her eyes, his expression troubled. "Are you sure? After what I—what we—?"

More than anything else she wanted sex with Jake one last time. She wanted to make peace with him, wanted this time to create a memory she could treasure. Most of all, it would help her forget that in a few hours, she would never see him again. Sass rose on tiptoe and kissed his mouth. "Yes," she whispered, "I'm sure."

So he undressed her a second time that day, but this time very gently. At the last moment he pulled the pins out of her hair and her bun came down. He gave a grunt of satisfaction that made her giggle in a watery way. Then they lay down to a very different sort of lovemaking—tender and infinitely sad. And even though it was different, once again Jake touched that part deep inside her. This time it was with love and a strange sense of completion that she abandoned herself to the long, sliding slope of ecstasy.

There wasn't much time left. She lay curled up in his arms, tracing circles on his chest. His hand stroked her shoulder.

"I'm sorry," she said.

"Yeah."

"It's my job. But I still believe I've made the right recommendation."

He sighed. "I know you do."

His voice was very, very sad.

CHAPTER TWENTY-FOUR

ON TUESDAY the following week, Rob phoned Jake. "The report has just been e-mailed through. Come over and we'll read it together."

Jake drove into Whangarimu with the strange calm that had settled over him since he'd watched Sass's plane disappear. The sun still shone, the waves were good, the boys fooled around as much as ever, but Jake was on autopilot. He put on a good act, though, and no one would have guessed he didn't taste the food he ate, didn't hear the movies he watched with the boys.

Rob met him at the door. "Come on in. I've printed out copies for us both."

He led the way into his office, where the two reports sat tidily on the desk.

"Any accompanying message?" Jake's tone was neutral as he picked one up and took a seat.

Rob shook his head. "The e-mail had a 'Hope you will look upon this proposal favorably' letter signed by that bastard Branston. I'd assumed he's taken over while Sass is with her mum, but I've just received a text from her."

Jake sat forward too quickly. "What did it say?"

"That's the weird thing. It's only a Web site."

"What the hell?"

"I know, but first things first. We'll read the report, then check out the site."

"Okay."

Jake tried to focus, but the words seemed to jump on the page. He could understand them, all right, but couldn't absorb them. It was as though this calm of his had robbed him not only of every emotion, but every coherent thought, too. He skimmed through the document, then tossed it back on the desk before prowling over to the window, where he propped his shoulder on the wall and looked out over Moana's riotous flower beds. It was so quiet he could hear the clock ticking. After what seemed an eternity he heard Rob lean back in his chair with a sigh.

"Well, what do you think?" Jake didn't turn around.

"To be honest, it's a lot better than I was expecting."

Jake jerked himself off the wall. "It's a resort, for crissakes." He went back to his chair and flung himself down, legs extended.

"An eco-resort," his brother countered. "A different proposition altogether. A different clientele. It'll attract those who genuinely care about the environment. It'll also be a smaller operation, far less intrusive."

"You can dress it up any way you like, a resort is still a resort."

Rob strummed the table with his fingers as he regarded his brother. "Yeah, got that. What we need now, Jake, is to focus on what to do next, and I could do with your help. Jacob's teething, so I've hardly slept and can't deal with your sulks right this moment."

Jake was suddenly aware of the dark rings under his brother's eyes, the unusual pallor of his skin.

"You look like shit."

Humor lit Rob's eyes. "Ditto, brother. What's your excuse?"

But Jake hardly knew where to begin. There was a short silence, then Rob said, "Come on, let's have a look at this Web site of Sass's."

"It'll be more mumbo jumbo about how great eco-resorts are," Jake muttered, but he pulled his chair around to Rob's side of the desk to look at the computer.

It was the site for a land-watch interest group in the States that uncovered unscrupulous business practices by major corporations. It had in its sights one particular development company that had been engaged in a running battle with a Native American group over a particular piece of land, and there were links to numerous articles about it.

The land in question was a sacred site, the scene of one of the bloodiest battles between the English forces and the Native Americans, and there had been vigorous opposition to a proposed subdivision. The campaign had been run along similar lines as the fairy tern protests—petitions, articles, a march. Yet despite all the indignation and fury, the proposed housing estate surged ahead. Then somehow *Sixty Minutes* got hold of the story and the whole campaign swung around.

Eminent academics called on the authorities to preserve places of historical significance. Native Americans demanded that once, just once, they deserved to be heard. This was followed by interviews with locals saying they could never feel comfortable living on the graves of massacred people. In the end the company backed down, issued an unreserved apology and gifted the land back to the people. A company spokesman was quoted on the importance of preserving sites significant to indigenous peoples.

After they'd scrolled down to the final article, the brothers sat back and stared at each other.

"What the hell's she playing at?" Jake asked. While he'd been reading the article, curiosity had flicked the switch and his brain had finally come back online. For the first time since Sass's departure he felt wired and alert.

"I don't know," said Rob. "It wasn't Sass's company in the limelight." He scratched his neck. "Is it linked to the fairy terns, d'you think?"

"I doubt it. Sass said that seven birds couldn't make the difference."

Anger burned in Jake's belly. Blessed anger. It was so good to *feel* again. He clutched at it and tried to remember how resentment felt, too. Funnily enough, neither one was that strong anymore.

"She does build in protcction for them, however," Rob pointed out. "First of all, the type of people who'll come to an eco-resort will respect the birds. Also by guaranteeing part of the profits would go into trying to save them, set up breeding programs, etc."

"Yeah, whatever. That still doesn't explain this." Jake pointed to the computer. "We're missing something."

"What?"

"I have no idea."

For a few minutes they just sat there. Then Jake snapped his fingers as he sat up straight. "The pa! A significant landmark of the indigenous people."

"She doesn't know anything about it, does she?"

"She spotted it the first day. Asked me questions. Man, she is *good.*" Despite everything, Jake couldn't help feeling admiration. "She kept her cards so close to her chest, I never guessed a thing. Even took her up there, told her the myth, some of the history. And all the time she just looked mildly interested, when she knew—she *knew*—it was a potential bomb. Having seen one company lose, she knew hers could, too." He sat back, shaking his head. "What a devious opponent."

"You sound proud of her."

Jake grinned. "I am. Crazy, eh?"

Rob narrowed his eyes. "Moana was right, then. There *were* sparks between you."

This sobered Jake. He dropped his eyes and muttered, "Yeah, there were. Didn't end well, though."

"Because you thought she was taking us for a ride?"

"Yeah. I assumed her report was a personal attack—go against my campaign, go against me." He smiled grimly. "She said I'd confuse business with us and I did."

"So you lost it over the report?"

Jake raised his eyes to meet his brother's sympathetic but still judicial gaze. "Yeah." He sighed. "What a stuff-up."

"Except that we've won," Rob pointed out. "You know the Maori department at Auckland University has been looking for money to excavate this site for years. Leak this to the press, get our own *Sixty Minutes* crew involved and we'll have an international incident in no time. You can just see the headlines—Bullying Americans Steal Heritage from Indigenous People."

"The resort she proposes isn't anywhere near the pa," Jake felt bound to mention.

"Doesn't matter. We stir up enough dust, enough emotion, no one's going to check the facts too carefully." Rob looked at Jake. "What's the problem, Jake? She's just handed us the silver bullet. Thanks to Sass, we're going to win."

CHAPTER TWENTY-FIVE

SASS PUT THE TWO polystyrene cups on the stand before sitting down beside her mother's hospital bed. She was pleased to note there was more color in Mom's cheeks today and that her sleep seemed peaceful. They had had a worrying week as their mother warred not only with the pneumonia, but alcohol withdrawal, too. A few days ago she'd turned a corner, in large part, the doctors said, to the care and support Sass and Adam were giving her.

Glancing across the bed, Sass saw her gorgeous young brother contorted on the hospital chair, gently snoring. She marveled that he could sleep in such a position, but it proved how exhausted he was. He was working construction at the moment, often pulling double shifts to help cover the added expenses. Sass had told him not to be ridiculous, she had money, but when she saw Adam's dark face flush, she could have bitten her tongue out.

"I *want* to do this for Mom. Okay by you, hotshot?"

She'd let the sarcasm ride. "Yeah, of course. I'm sorry, not thinking straight. It'll be great to go shares."

It was funny how this crisis had pulled the family together after all these years. Even Cole was doing his bit, writing letters and sending drawings of life in prison. Sass had forgotten how he'd always drawn as a kid. The sketches could have been grim, but Cole had a way of capturing the human moments: men playing cards, a guard and a prisoner sharing a joke. The one of a huge, tattooed lifer holding bread out to a bird was pinned up on the wall. It made Mom smile when she looked at it.

A trolley rumbled past the door and Adam stirrcd, his eyes flickering open. From the time he'd been born, he'd had the most beautiful eyes—black, so deep you could lose yourself in them, and eyelashes that were the envy of his big sister. He smiled, his lean face lighting up.

"Hey, Sass." With a groan he uncoiled and ran a hand through his midnight hair, thick, dead straight and floppy in a way that even a sister could see was madly sexy. No wonder their mother was getting excellent treatment from all the nurses.

He stretched his arms over his head, groaning again. "God, that feels good."

"Here." Sass handed him one of the cups.

"Thanks." His voice was still groggy and in a few gulps, he dispensed with the coffee.

"How can you drink that fast? Especially when it's so disgusting."

He laughed shortly. "Life on the road means you take what you are given with no complaints." He gestured to the bed with his chin. "She slept easy all night, far as I can tell."

Sass smiled and leaned forward to stroke their mom's hair. "She's looking so much better."

As though in response to that feather touch, Alicia's eyes drifted open. Seeing both children there, she smiled and reached out a hand, which Sass immediately took.

"Hey, there, Mom. Had a good sleep?"

"Why, very nice, thank you."

Sass smiled. Jake had teased her about her accent, but he'd be completely bowled over by her mother's way of speaking—like something right out of a 1930s movie. Then, as it always did when she thought of Jake—which was often—a wave of pain swept over her. But she tried to push it away.

She had so much to be grateful for in regaining her family like this, it seemed downright churlish to feel like a piece was still missing. Strangely, she didn't feel at all bad about having quit her job.

Alicia's eyes fell on her youngest child. "Adam Walker, you look like a cat dragged you backward through the bushes. You need to get home to your bed, young man."

He laughed as he rose and stretched again, his long arms almost knocking the overhead light.

"Watch out, klutz," Sass said automatically.

"Yeah, yeah," Adam retorted. "You just watch who you callin' klutz, lady, or you'll be out on the street on your ass."

"Threat or promise?"

"Children, children." But Alicia was smiling.

"I gotta go, Mom, and have a shower before work. See you tonight." Adam kissed her, then flicked a hand at his sister as he picked up his motorcycle helmet. "Thanks for the coffee."

"'Sa pleasure. I've stocked up on toilet paper and there are clean clothes on your bed."

He grinned. "I just love having a live-in housekeeper."

"Ha, you say that now. You moaned enough about it when I first moved in."

"That's because you meddled with my stuff."

"It's called *cleaning*, Adam."

"Whatever. Catch you tonight."

"Don't be late, I'm cooking chicken."

He gave her a thumbs-up and went into the corridor, where they could hear him say, "Oops, I surely do apologize for nearly running you down, Miz Nurse."

Sass and her mother exchanged glances as they heard the responding giggles.

"That boy has more charm than any individual has any right to," Alicia said.

"He's incorrigible," Sass agreed. "But I'll say this for him, he doesn't take advantage of it as much as he could."

Alicia smiled. "He's a good boy." Then her eyes welled with tears. "They're both good boys and I failed them so badly."

In her weakened state, Alicia was very emotional and, having been sober for two weeks now, was thinking straighter than she had in years.

"I don't deserve any of you."

"Hush, Mom, don't say that. You did your best. All we want now is for you to get better. The doctor says you should be out in just a few days. Then you can go into the clinic, where they say you'll be treated like royalty." She tapped the nicotine patch on her own arm. "We Walker women are going to kick our addictions together."

Alicia reached for Sass's hand again. Her grip was surprisingly strong for a frail woman. "Are you sure you've got the money for the clinic, sweetheart? I don't want to use up your life savings."

Sass laughed. "Mom, I've already told you, I worked like a slave for seven years and now I want to have fun."

"Paying for your mother's rehabilitation isn't fun."

"But it will be," Sass assured her, stroking her mother's fingers, "soon as you get out. We'll do things together and maybe persuade Adam to stick around. Cole will be out of prison next year and we'll be a family again."

Her mother gave her a searching look. "Sasha, don't go making too many plans for us. After all, the boys are their own men now. Are you sure you aren't just wanting a family of your own?"

Caught off guard, Sass laughed uncertainly. "I don't know what you're talking about, Mom."

Of course, she should have realized if anyone could tell she was hiding something, it would be her mother.

"Do you want to tell me about it, baby?"

For a second, Sass actually considered denying it all. She knew Alicia would back off if she did. But if they were ever going to be a family again, she had to be strong enough to be vulnerable.

Taking a deep breath she said, "I fell in love with the wrong guy."

"Oh, baby, do I know how that one feels," Alicia said. Sass pulled her chair close to the bed and rested her head on the sheets, surrendering to her mother's stroking fingers.

"Tell me," said Alicia, and so the story tumbled out. It sounded garbled as she told her mom about Aroha Bay with its boys and birds, about Rob and Moana and taking the drop. But when it came to talking about Jake, she faltered. She just couldn't seem to find the right words to describe him: the way he made her madder than she'd ever been, but also the happiest, the craziest. That started her crying, and for a while she sobbed into the sheets, while Alicia continued to smooth her hair and make the same sympathetic noises she used to when Sass was a kid and hurt herself. It was wonderfully soothing, and finally Sass sat upright and blew her nose.

"The stupid thing is," she said, "he's all wrong for me, but I just can't stop thinking about him."

"Are you sure he's so wrong for you? He sounds pretty good to me."

Sass shook her head. "He hates me, Mom." She tried to smile. "Sorry for the scene."

Alicia's own smile was blinding. "Sasha, I'm glad—not of your pain, not *at all*—but that you let me be a mother again. You shut yourself away when you were twelve." She touched Sass on the cheek. "You were the cutest but most headstrong little thing I ever did see—all long skinny legs and uncompromising beliefs. I've never met any other living being with as much boneheaded determination as you."

Sass laughed. "That's because you haven't met Jake Finlayson."

At that moment, a nurse popped her head around the door. "Morning, Mrs. Walker. Time for your shower."

Sass kissed her mom's cheek. "I'll get coffee."

She prowled down the corridors until she came to the cafeteria. It was a bright room, but sterile and cheerless. She stood in front of the glass cabinets staring at the plastic-looking doughnuts, polystyrene sandwiches and Frisbee-size cookies. In the end, she settled for a diet Dr Pepper. Funny that, they didn't have Dr Pepper in New Zealand.

Sass put her elbows on the table, buried her face in her hands and dug her fingers into her scalp. Oh God, she had to stop this obsession with New Zealand. Talking about Jake hadn't helped at all. It had brought him back too vividly and she was driving herself crazy. She pressed the heels of her hands hard into her eye sockets, determined to stop more damned tears from spilling down her face.

Behind her she heard the purposeful footsteps of someone on a mission. Lucky person. Intellectually, she knew she was on the right path—only, her heart seemed to have lost the way. As the footsteps came close, they slowed.

"This seat taken?"

The voice was deep. The accent was Kiwi. She really was going crazy if she was beginning to hallucinate. She slowly dropped her hands and stared up in disbelief.

"Jake?"

CHAPTER TWENTY-SIX

HIS SMILE WAS UNCERTAIN—not a trace of the cocky surfer there. "Can I sit with you?" He seemed…almost humble. Surely not. Not Jake.

"Of course." She gestured to the chair.

His eyes were as green as she remembered, the hair as wild. He was dressed in worn jeans, a jersey and a beat-up bomber jacket. She'd never seen him wearing so many clothes. But it was his expression that was most unfamiliar. For the first time ever, he seemed unsure of himself.

"I've had one hell of a runaround trying to track you down," he told her. "You've changed your phone number."

Despite feeling dazed, she couldn't help smiling at the severity in his voice. "Yeah, I handed my phone in when I quit the company. I've got this now."

She fished in her pocket and pulled out a cell phone that was the very humble cousin of her

BlackBerry. She liked it. Its pared-down functionality suited her new pared-down life.

Jake shook his head. "Well, that certainly made my job a lot harder. Do you have any idea how many Walkers live in this city? I decided to visit the hospitals rather than start ringing every Walker listed. Problem was, I don't know your mother's first name. The accent didn't help. One hospital even called Security."

Sass laughed, unable to believe this was really happening. "So how did you find me here?"

"I finally lucked out. Just as I got to the information desk, this dangerous-looking guy carrying a motorbike helmet walks past, flips a hand at the nurses and says, 'Bye, y'all, see you tonight. Have a nice day now.' They all giggled and called back, 'Bye now, Mr. Walker.' I knew it had to be Adam. His smile is just like yours. The lovely woman at the desk sent me to your mother's room."

"You didn't go in!"

"I knocked first," he assured her.

"What did Mom say?"

He smiled. "She looks like you. She has your eyes. She took one look and said, 'Why, it's Jake, I do believe. How very nice to meet you, but don't stop now. Sass is in the cafeteria.' And so—" he spread his hands "—here I am."

"What about the boys? Where are they?"

His eyes held that glint of mischief she'd thought she'd never see again. "Mum and Dad have moved in for the time being."

"No!" Sass couldn't help answering his grin with one of her own. "How's that going?"

"Judging by the number of aggrieved texts I've received from the kids, I gather the old man is having a fine time inducting them into the Finlayson world of pull-your-socks-up-and-just-bloody-get-on-with-it."

There were so many thoughts, so many feelings, but all she could do was sit with a stupid smile spread over her face.

"It's good to see you," Jake said, then stopped. "Oh, as I was leaving, Moana told me that as soon as I said, 'It's good to see you,' I had to remind you of Kiwispeak. I told her that I wouldn't be saying anything so lame to the woman I loved, but there, I just did."

Something very close to happiness fizzed deep inside Sass as she said, "You love me?"

"Of course. I've come to take you back."

It took all her strength not to throw herself at him crying, *yes yes yes.* There was a lot of stuff they needed to sort out between them. "First I need to know why you didn't play the pa card." Seeing his quizzical expression, she added, "Yeah, I know the resort is going ahead unopposed. I saw it on the ABORD site." Feeling suddenly shy, she confessed, "I check Whangarimu out on the net, most nights."

Jake's tone was mock-severe as he said, "Before I answer your question, I want to know why you sent the text in the first place. You tried sabotaging your own company."

"No, I didn't," Sass assured him. "I'd already resigned. Although I did use their phone one last time. I felt bad about that but I didn't have my new phone and knew you'd be getting the report any minute. Did it arrive in time?"

"It did, but why did you send it? Remorse?"

"No!" She tucked her hair behind her ear. "I will always believe I made the right call, but it only seemed fair for you guys to have the option of blocking the resort if, after everything, you still didn't want it. So did Rob talk you out of it?"

He leaned back in his chair. "It was the other way around, actually. Initially I was mad as hell, but once I'd read your report properly, I could see it made sense—especially for the community. Rob tried to persuade me we could win. Said you wanted us to or you wouldn't have sent the text. He twisted all my arguments, but once I'd decided, I remained adamant."

"But why would Rob…?"

"Well, at first I thought the Finlayson need to win

was clouding his judgment, but later I realized he was just playing me. I think he learned about reverse psychology from his wife. By making me defend and rationalize all your decisions, I could become entirely sure of what I thought should happen."

"And what is that?" She searched his eyes.

"You were right. The report was separate from the two of us. Taking egos out, I think you made the right call. There's tremendous excitement in Whangarimu about it. Your company has also been loud in its assurances that it will be the most eco-friendly resort ever built. It's to be their flagship for good relations. They are even more hell-bent than us on saving the tern now."

He shot her a wicked smile. "Actually, your text meant we could accept the report with the proviso that some profits also go toward the pa excavation. Your company loved that idea and is now talking about a recreation of a Maori village, too. Win-win."

He exuded the smug satisfaction of a warrior well pleased with the outcome of a battle. Sass laughed and Jake stretched out his hands to catch hers. "Come home with me. We need you. Your company would love someone like you on that end, and the boys miss you. Moana is furious that you left without saying goodbye, though she understands. Manu said to tell you he wants you to run for mayor. You've got to come."

Sass couldn't speak for the emotion overwhelming her. But then she pulled her hands away. "I can't. There's Mom, and Adam and Cole. We're trying to be a family again."

"I guessed as much when I heard you'd quit your job." He leaned forward. "Was it a hard decision?"

She felt herself blush under his intent scrutiny. It felt so good to be the object of his fierce attention again.

"A no-brainer," she assured him. His head tipped, a silent invitation for her to elaborate. "Flying home, I started questioning my priorities. Being likened to my father hurt." She grimaced. "All the more because there was some truth in it. Having all those hours in the air gave me time to think about what I wanted in the future. Fearing for Mom, being so grateful to Adam for being there for her, hating myself for not—" Sass broke off.

"So?" Jake prompted.

This guy never gave her a break. "So," she said, looking directly at him, "I figured if some surf champ could throw away his whole career in search of something more meaningful, I could do the same."

Jake grabbed one of her hands. "Really? Because of me?"

His grip was strong, his palm warm. "Yeah, because of you." Sass felt strangely shy, but realized she was finally learning to do deep-and-meaningfuls, and smiled. "I missed you guys so much. The kids and the place had me on day one."

He laughed. "Then come back."

"I can't, I've got ties here."

"Bring them with you."

The absurdity of that statement made her laugh, but Jake seized her other hand and held both tight as he leaned over the table. "It doesn't have to be immediately, Sass. You can stay until your mum is well again, then bring her to New Zealand temporarily. Adam can come out for a holiday, too. You know us…" His grin regained the cockiness she remembered so well. "we'll wow them with the scenery and charm. It's happened before."

"Yeah, but maybe they won't be quite the pushover I was." More seriously she added, "It's crazy. I can't just drop my mom and brother on you, even if I could persuade them to come down to New Zealand. You guys might not get along."

She didn't really believe that. Jake and Adam would hit it off well. And everyone loved Alicia. But still…

Jake shook his head at what he clearly saw as silliness. "They're family, Sass. They can't drive me any crazier than my father does. If you guys want to be together, great. If not, that's fine, too. Nothing has to be tied down. Life is messy and we'll work it out as we go along." He smiled, but his expression was sincere. "I just want you, whatever."

Her heart tripped into the tattoo it beat only around him. *Are you sure you don't just want a family of your own?*

With that, Jake shoved his chair back and jerked Sass up and into a hard embrace, kissing her not at all gently, but very thoroughly. Suddenly he broke off the kiss.

"What the—?"

His fingers were at the top of her arm, under the sleeve of her loose jersey. He looked at her, laughter in his eyes. "Is that a patch I've just found, Miss Pain-in-the?"

"It is," she said primly. "Mother and I are going to kick our addictions together."

He threw back his head and laughed. "You, Sass, are my addiction. But I have every intention of overdosing every day for the rest of my life."

And that, she concluded, was the closest she'd ever get in Kiwispeak to a declaration of undying, deep and passionate love.

"Good enough," she replied.

* * * * *

Harlequin offers a romance for every mood!
See below for a sneak peek
from our paranormal romance line,
Silhouette® Nocturne™.
Enjoy a preview of REUNION by USA TODAY
bestselling author Lindsay McKenna.

Aella closed her eyes and sensed a distinct shift, like movement from the world around her to the unseen world.

She opened her eyes. And had a slight shock at the man standing ten feet away. He wasn't just any man. Her heart leaped and pounded. He reminded her of a fierce warrior from an ancient civilization. Incan? She wasn't sure but she felt his deep power and masculinity.

I'm Aella. Are you the guardian of this sacred site? she asked, hoping her telepathy was strong.

Fox's entire body soared with joy. Fox struggled to put his personal pleasure aside.

Greetings, Aella. I'm the assistant guardian to

this sacred area. You may call me Fox. How can I be of service to you, Aella? he asked.

I'm searching for a green sphere. A legend says that the Emperor Pachacuti had seven emerald spheres created for the Emerald Key necklace. He had seven of his priestesses and priests travel the world to hide these spheres from evil forces. It is said that when all seven spheres are found, restrung and worn, that Light will return to the Earth. The fourth sphere is here, at your sacred site. Are you aware of it? Aella held her breath. She loved looking at him, especially his sensual mouth. The desire to kiss him came out of nowhere.

Fox was stunned by the request. *I know of the Emerald Key necklace because I served the emperor at the time it was created. However, I did not realize that one of the spheres is here.*

Aella felt sad. Why? Every time she looked at Fox, her heart felt as if it would tear out of her chest. *May I stay in touch with you as I work with this site?* she asked.

Of course. Fox wanted nothing more than to be here with her. To absorb her ephemeral beauty and hear her speak once more.

Aella's spirit lifted. What *was* this strange connection between them? Her curiosity was strong, but she had more pressing matters. In the next few days, Aella knew her life would change forever. How, she had no idea….

Look for REUNION
by USA TODAY *bestselling author*
Lindsay McKenna,
available April 2010,
only from Silhouette® Nocturne™.